Praise for *Speak, Silence*

"[P]owerful . . . an incredibly forceful book that insists readers sit up and pay attention; despite the gains made with the Foča trial, most of us continue to turn a blind eye to abuses taking place around the world. With [*Speak, Silence*], Echlin demands more of us." —*Quill & Quire*, starred review

"Through a story of tragedy and community rebuilding, *Speak, Silence* hooks the reader from the beginning to the last page. . . . In an impeccably well-researched text, Kim Echlin portrays the horrors of the Bosnian war through the stories of systemic sexual assault in three generations of a Muslim family. With prose that portrays both horror and hope, Echlin takes the reader on a journey that follows women of all ages as they force the world to acknowledge for the first time that rape is not only a crime against an individual, it is also a crime against humanity." —2021 Toronto Book Awards Jury

"[A] necessary novel. . . . *Speak, Silence* is a bridge between those purely fictional stories of women's trauma at the hands of men, and the purely non-fiction books about the war crime of rape. . . . [Y]ou need to read this book." —*Toronto Star*

"Echlin's books, difficult as their subjects can be, are much more than worth the pain. Beyond their considerable literary merit and pleasure, they offer a richer, deeper, truer entrée than non-fiction can provide into happenings we would often prefer to ignore. They give us a peerless c
Review of Canada

"Writing about living through a war draws on some of our most volatile emotions and fears—the balance between trauma and sensationalism is a precarious one. Writing about the rage and humiliation of women raped in war takes this already precarious balance several degrees further. *Speak, Silence* ushers us into a community of women who guide us with sensitivity, clarity and love through their resistance to being stereotyped as victims." —Ellen Elias-Bursac, translator of South Slavic languages and author of *Translating Evidence and Interpreting Testimony at a War Crimes Tribunal*

"Between 1991 and 1995, an estimated 60,000 women were raped in wars in the former Yugoslavia. But the women did not allow these rapes to become an historical footnote or 'collateral damage.' They witnessed their ordeal in The Hague's International Tribunal. Thanks to these women, the world understood—for the first time—rape as a weapon of war and found the accused guilty of a Crime Against Humanity. This carefully researched and well-crafted novel, based on these true events, is an impressive monument to the women." —Slavenka Drakulić, journalist and author of *They Would Never Hurt a Fly*

"[*Speak, Silence*] is a testament both to empathy and also to its limits. . . . It's brutal in a sense, but just as beautiful, Echlin embodying both-ness again by making death-and-violence and undying love both absolutely true at once." —Kerry Clare, author of *Mitzi Bytes* and *Waiting for a Star to Fall*

Speak, Silence

KIM ECHLIN

PENGUIN

an imprint of Penguin Canada,
a division of Penguin Random House Canada Limited

First published in Hamish Hamilton hardcover, 2021

Published in this edition, 2022

1 2 3 4 5 6 7 8 9 10

Publisher's note: This book is a work of fiction. Names, characters, places and incidents either
are the product of the author's imagination or are used fictitiously, and any resemblance to actual
persons living or dead, events, or locales is entirely coincidental.

Excerpt from *Jean Améry, At the Mind's Limits: Contemplations by a Survivor on Auschwitz and
Its Realities*. Published by Indiana University Press, Bloomington, IN, copyright © 1990 and used
with permission cleared with Copyright Clearance Centre. Excerpt from Mehmedalija "Mak"
Dizdar, "Calypso", adapted from the English translation copyright © 2006 by Keith Doubt and
Luisa Lang Owen, and used with permission from the Dizdar Estate. Excerpt from *Calling the
Ghosts: a Story About Rape, War and Women*, quote by Jadranka Cigelj. Directed by Mandy
Jacobson and Karmen Jelincic with executive producer Julia Ormond, distributed by Women
Make Movies. www.wmm.com.

LIBRARY AND ARCHIVES CANADA CATALOGUING IN PUBLICATION

Title: Speak, silence / Kim Echlin.
Names: Echlin, Kim, author.
Description: Previously published: Toronto: Hamish Hamilton Canada, 2021.
Identifiers: Canadiana 20200233823 | ISBN 9780735240636 (softcover)
Classification: LCC PS8559.C45 S64 2022 | DDC C813/.54—dc23

Cover and book design by Kate Sinclair
Cover images: (leaves) Alpine Buckthorn from *Traité des Arbres et Arbustes que l'on cultive en
France en pleine terre* (1801-1819) by Pierre-Joseph Redouté. Original from the New York Public
Library. Digitally enhanced by rawpixel; (flowers) from *Iconographie du genre camellia: No. 194*
(1839-1843), published by Abbé Laurent Berlèse. Gift of The Print Club of Cleveland in honour
of Mrs. William G. Mather / The Cleveland Museum of Art.

Printed in the United States of America

www.penguinrandomhouse.ca

Penguin
Random House
PENGUIN CANADA

for the women who testified

for Nicole Winstanley

. . . he sat down and lit a cigarette, and he said that he could perhaps do more, much more, but that I was about the same age as his daughter, and so he wouldn't do anything more for the moment.

—*protected witness*

A Note on the Novel

In 2000 a landmark trial took place in The Hague. The Foča case was in response to the thousands of rapes that took place during the Yugoslav wars (1992 to 1999) in centres set up as rape camps. Prosecutors needed six years to prepare for the trial. An international team of women lawyers and researchers travelled around the world to find women witnesses, now war refugees, who dared to testify. The trial lasted for nine months.

The International Tribunal for the Former Yugoslavia (ICTY) was born out of Nuremberg's remnant hope for enduring international justice. Judges were appointed from fifty-two nations. Nine hundred people from around the globe worked in the courts. The ICTY was established in 1993 to contest violations of international humanitarian law. Many trials took place *during* the wars.

The Foča trial in 2000 asked us to agree that never again would a woman's body be used as a theatre of war. But always we say never again. To this day women are systematically raped as part of terror and war.

Important new jurisprudence came out of the Foča trial. The perpetrators were found guilty, not only of rape but of a crime against humanity. For the first time in 5,000 years of recorded history women were not spoils of war. Rape in war was no longer a crime against individual women but a crime against all of us.

Speak, Silence is an imaginative response, in fiction, to changing consciousness. Let us reimagine our humanity together.

—KE

Toronto, Sarajevo

They are still shooting, said Jacques Payac.

I'm going, I said. The borders are open.

I run a travel magazine, he said.

I will write a travel piece.

About war?

About film.

When the hell are you going to settle down?

Why should I settle down?

What are you hoping for?

I only want to know. To tell.

I HAD WATCHED the war on television in Toronto for years. I watched life in a city under siege, saw people from a bread line bleeding on the ground. The cameras pulled back and I saw smoke and fire from apartment towers. My name is Gota Dobson. I saw these images on the same screen that I watched Looney Tunes with my only child. Intolerable shame. To watch old women in good leather shoes hurrying over rubble along the edges of buildings. To watch boys and girls playing on tanks. To watch people falling like broken clay pigeons in skeet practice. To change the channel. To live in the unattended moment. To be where I was not.

There was the *Time* cover of a crowd of prisoners behind wire fences, their ribs like empty cages, with a caption in red: *Must It Go On?* The war did not abate and the news remained clear and constant and the world struggled to rouse itself.

People knew. Still it went on. Year after year I watched. When Biddy was asleep at night and my work was put away for another day, I watched.

To know is not enough.

SO I WENT to Sarajevo to write about the film festival when they were still fighting outside the city. They ran the projectors off car batteries. Someone asked, Why are you holding a film festival in the middle of a war? The director answered, Why are they holding a war in the middle of a film festival?

I saw the Sarajevo roses in the sidewalks, the pockmarks on the walls. The city was alive with the temporary glamour of international film stars gathering in war ruins. Where was the rage? On the streets I heard wry humour and relief. I felt mourning. Exhaustion.

I asked at the Sartr Theatre box office, Do you know a man called Kosmos?

Yes, said the young woman.

Does he have another name?

She thought for a moment and said, Everyone calls him Kosmos.

I left an envelope for him. Inside was a note in which I told him I would meet him that night at the Kino Bosna. I had not seen him for eleven years.

—

THE ANNOUNCEMENT OF a new court in The Hague had spread quickly around the globe. They would need judges, litigators, researchers, interpreters. They would write a new set of rules and procedures. They wanted to bring order into that lawless place, the border.

In Hamburg, Karla Vogel-Babić applied to be a prosecutor. She was married to a man from the region. Her specialty was international white-collar crime but she was tired of the greed. When she was a child she had lost her home in the rubble of her war-flattened city. She knew the smell of decomposing corpses. She wanted to be part of this new thing, a world court. A woman has no country and wants no country. Borders shift and crack into something different.

Other women in other places were also deciding to leave their homes to go to The Hague. They too wanted to act. They too felt their home to be the world.

In Lusaka, the deputy chief justice told Judge Gladys Banda that the United Nations was looking for African judges. At first Gladys thought she could not fit in with international lawyers. She had five children but this had never stopped her from doing new work. Her husband encouraged her and she thought, All the new judges will have to learn the new law too. She had learned how to navigate Zambian tradition and British common law. Perhaps there were things she could do.

All over the world, people were weighing the idea of joining the new court. History is now. In the moment of consciousness. New law on the border.

—

THE KINO BOSNA café was converted from a cinema, seats replaced with tables and red-checked cloths, and on the walls classic black-and-white photos of old Hollywood stars, Bogart and Hepburn and Monroe. The smoke-filled room was full of young students whose educations had been interrupted, laughing through their war trauma, trying to invent a retro-present in a city besieged for three years, ten months, three weeks and three days. They crowded round a game of chess and mocked missteps, called out things like *The chicken has laid a potato*. For the young, hope is as natural as violence. They played U2 and Sikter and Protest. They joked, *You think one president is difficult? Try three, a Bosniak, a Croat and a Serb.* But it was not a joke.

Goat?

Kosmos.

He sat at a table with a woman. His hair fell over his left eye, and he moved with that familiar kinetic energy. He was pulling over a chair and saying, What are you doing here? In his eyes the ironic distance and intimate warmth I remembered, and I felt all over again blood pulsing beneath my skin. I loved all over again his lifted eyebrows.

He said, This is Edina, and she looked up, politely, was chain-smoking, did not speak. I wondered if she had no English. Her face was sallow, her bony fingers long, the skin around her lips a dry net of wrinkles. Some of her hair was tucked behind her right ear. She had once been pretty. Her shifting grey-blue eyes were more alive than her flesh, her energy an erect snake waiting to strike.

He was talking fast. He said that he had stayed away from Sarajevo for too long, could I not hear his British accent, was it not fucked up, and was not British English boring, their insults boring, nothing interesting like fuck my python.

He was a little uneasy.

Finally he asked, You?

I said, I have a daughter. I write. I came for the festival.

I thought, I came to see you.

He said, I was working at a small theatre in London, near a church, oranges and lemons, when the war started, and I did not come back. I thought I would go crazy watching the war on television, waiting, like waiting for fucking Godot.

His charming soup of language. But Edina leaned back, detached from his I-wasn't-here-during-the-war stories.

He said, This festival is only for movie stars, in and out like a quickie. I am living here now. There was nothing for me over there.

I wanted to be alone with him. To ask him what really happened. Now I had seen him again, I wanted to touch him.

I asked Edina, Are you in theatre too?

I am a lawyer. But I do not practise.

Kosmos said, She works with women from the war.

What do you do?

Abruptly Edina rose, walked into the crowded room.

I looked at Kosmos. He said, Sometimes she has to get up and move away. When she feels trapped it is better to move. It is difficult for her to talk about what happened.

But I asked her about her work, I said.

It is the same, said Kosmos. She runs a documentation centre. She takes statements from women about what happened in the war.

I thought, Terrible things happened.

I asked, Does she have family?

Her daughter and mother live in Vienna.

Where is her husband? I asked.

Dead.

We watched Edina standing with a small group of people across the room near a chess game. She laughed with them over some absurd chess insult, came back to the table, reached for a cigarette, lit it, and called the waiter to order cakes for us. She flicked her cigarette ashes on the floor. I could see that she had once been a woman who was lively at parties, smoking and calling for food and moving easily through crowded rooms. She took everything in. I hesitated to say anything more, but Kosmos, who was never comfortable with silence, said to her, Maybe Goat could write about your work, help raise money.

Always he had ideas. The waiters began to pile chairs on tables and people moved out through the front doors into the early morning. Still Edina sat. The waiters wiped the bar and mopped the floors around us and Edina drew her hands over her face, which seemed to soothe her. Then she turned to me.

I do not ask for their stories, she said. I beg for them. I document where a woman was taken and what happened to her and who in her family died and where survivors went after the war and how they live. They all need money. The women can't support themselves.

I nodded.

She said, I want to prosecute.

Her body was intense and strangely vulnerable though she was a tall woman. There was a subtle fierceness in the way she held her back and her eyes were ball lightning.

She said, People have heard about my work. Some women

from the international court are coming. But what can they really do? I want prosecution *here*.

She squashed her last cigarette and twisted the empty package and said, Shit. We are all betrayed. The world forgets us.

Turn aside this fate, you gods.

Kosmos offered her one of his cigarettes and she let him cup her hand while he lit it.

She reached into her bag of files and papers and she pulled out a photocopy of a newspaper photograph of women standing in a room together. She wrote something in the margin, crumpled the paper and handed it to me. She got up and Kosmos stood to follow her.

She said, They just wait for us to die.

I WATCHED THEM leave and waited to pay the bill. They were out on the sidewalk and Kosmos hurried back, leaned in close and asked, Where are you staying?

I told him to come to my hotel in the old town. Everyone knew it. And then I walked through the narrow streets toward the old bazaar, blood-tainted since the Illyrian wars. The moon was very low and early dawn light was grey over the rough cobbles and there were many doorways and places to hide. Listening to Edina had shredded me like a grater. I looked at the wall of white names carved into red stone in the Markale fresh market. Vendors with dark smudges under their eyes were setting up tables of vegetables and fruit, figs and breads and honey under the names of the dead. Was a memorial a final deletion, so war could be put aside, so trade and life could proceed?

The bar downstairs at the Hotel Art was lit with Ottoman-style lanterns, and behind the mustard columns and stone tiles was enough cheap alcohol to poison an army. Three men were still drinking, heads and necks jutting forward like gargoyle downspouts. I asked for water. And the oldest man stood and handed me a blue bottle to take up three flights of stairs to my room. I opened the door to a pair of narrow twin beds with wrought-iron headboards and took a long drink of water. Outside, the river, and all across the valley, red rooftops and white buildings, minarets a breath taller than nearby church spires, then the forest on the ridge of the mountain. We are pack animals and live close to each other, even hunters and hunted nestle together in the bowl of the valley. Below my window were stone traces of the market where Venetian traders once bartered in twelve thousand stalls, five centuries old. They held their lovers at night. They prayed. They played with their children. They gossiped about politicians threatening war. They bought and sold the things people want—spices, a bit of cloth, a pot, a carpet. Nothing is more human than trade, worship and war.

I flattened Edina's ball of paper. Dawn light outside the window was like spring water on young skin. No one would shoot from the hills today. The photocopy was printed in thin ink, grey-toned and pink-lined, like an old fresco. She had written her telephone number across the top. The women in the photo were together waiting. See them. Arms bare. Hair rough-cropped or tied or tangled and falling into their eyes. Hands clasped across their own arms over breasts and rubbing tears from cheeks. See them together waiting, flesh against flesh, waiting women, waiting for bread, for water, for children, for old men.

They had once been war-waiting, and they had survived. You would not abuse stone like that. Now they were peace-waiting. Ready to speak.

The photo caption calls them war victims. They make their necessary migration, guided not by winds or magnetic poles but by uncoded weather inside their bodies. They are grief-touching skin to skin, over there, see one woman holding another, and there in that corner, see a young woman squatting to the floor, head dropped between her knees. Flesh once soul-stripped but alive and not silent. They do not seem to be victims to me. See us. Listen to us.

Justice is a long-feathered, cragged old mountain bird. Under its stiff wings lice crawl, laying and hatching in the worn cycle of revenge and fear. In the ancient first language, the priestess prayed to her goddess and she was tossed by war, torn by thorns, and exiled. No home, no temple, she was left with nothing but her song under the light of planets. Verdicts do not undo waiting.

He knocked and I let him in. Of course. Now we were alone, not the tender and curious young strangers who first met in an unheated room in Paris, but two people who had not seen each other for many years.

He said, Our daughter must be eleven now.

You know about her?

I got the letter you sent to London.

You never answered.

He looked down.

Why?

His back was to the window. Over his shoulder I saw distant lights, people awakening across the valley.

He asked, Have you told her about me?

We sat facing each other on two single beds.

Of course. Since she was little. I told her there was a war. I said someday we would find you. Anyway, it was easier to raise her without you.

Goat.

I had no choice.

No.

Are you with Edina?

She only lets me be her friend. War destroyed everything.

How destroyed?

She lost everything. Her husband. Her father. Friends. Her life.

You still love her.

She does not love me. She has never loved me.

He reached for my hand.

I said, We have been up all night.

We used to like all night.

The warm flesh of his palm on the back of my hand.

I said, I still like all night.

I wanted to know things about him and I wanted to touch him as if we had never been apart. I wanted truth but I did not want pain. I could not have truth without pain.

I wanted him but I was also angry. I wanted this moment but I did not trust it.

I asked, Have you had many lovers?

He looked into my eyes with a little humour and with great gentleness and he said, It has been eleven years. Not many. Have you?

Yes, I said. But I wanted to say, I had a child. Ours.

He wanted to coax us back toward warmth, and he touched my leg and asked, Is this okay?

I said, I don't know if we should make love.

We have a daughter together, he said.

Always the way he spoke made me laugh. Time out of mind, a lover's brain.

I stood, pulled the curtain across the window, and now we were unhurried because something had been decided and he looked on the bed at the crumpled paper she had given me and he said, She wrote her number for you?

I came back and stood behind him and put my arms around him and said, Yes she did. I will lock the door.

And after I hung up the sign outside, *Ne ometaj*, I asked, Shall I call her?

He did not answer but took off my clothes, and I took off his, and we made love and I remembered the hungry joy of our months in Paris. But he had betrayed me and there had not yet been time for understanding or forgiveness though my body had already forgiven him because a body knows only what it feels in every moment. We were not in a yellow-lit city of love where neither of us belonged but in his war-forlorn country. We made love haunted by our past and by Edina, and by her dead beloved husband too, each of us loving the wrong one. We were tattered things, and foolish and lost. And there was also a child. A mother must reckon with the life she creates. And so, with the measure we used, our story would be measured to us.

After, we talked about London, about Toronto, about Biddy. Then we made love again, and this time it was deep and slow, and with our bodies we told each other the truth.

—

PEOPLE KNEW WHAT was happening to the women in that war. But there was never a magazine cover of a woman looking into a camera with clothes ripped, breasts cut, blood running down the insides of her thighs. There was no cover for this kind of victim of war. The places where women were locked up were called not prison camps but motels and schools and recreation centres. Women who survived that war were not called heroes. They were hidden.

Rise, unhappy woman, cries Hecuba, *all gone.* No longer queen but coin. Spoils of war.

Epics sing battle in words so lovely they shimmer over stench and pain. I think of the poor boy Harpalion, the spear's hideous wound between his genitals and navel, at the right buttock, under the bone, into the bladder, the boy gasping out his life, lying like a worm extended along the ground, dark blood drenching the earth, the boy-corpse lifted into a chariot and brought in sorrow to his father.

No poet has tenderly described insult to the vagina and womb and bowels of a woman. No poet makes a word-monument to a woman fighting naked, biting and kicking, beaten to silence, and nine months later, naked again, legs open again, giving birth to a child whose life began in rape. A woman's war is not redeemed for the ages by art.

Her suffering is meant to stir honour in the speeches of generals, *Let no man hurry to sail for home until he has raped a faithful Trojan wife, payment for the shock of war.* Her brave battle has no voice at all.

We embalm her in silent shame.

—

KOSMOS WAS GONE when I awoke in the late afternoon and I thought, This is complicated.

Our love was storm-tossed. Seeing him again was a sip of cool water.

I telephoned the number Edina had given me and she asked, Do you play chess?

Her office building was in a residential part of the city, apartments over barren main-floor rooms behind locked doors. Locks everywhere. I knocked and knocked and finally a young woman came out and let me in and we walked up some stairs and Edina was in an office with an elderly woman. I turned the pages of magazines in a language I could not read. After Edina walked with the old woman to the door, she came back to me and said, You came.

Yes. Will you show me your work?

Did you sleep with him?

Yes.

He sleeps with anyone.

She was pulling a file out of a drawer and she said, I knew him before the war.

I sat in the chair in front of her desk and said, When I met him in Paris, years ago, he told me about you on the first day. He only thinks of you.

She said, I will show you our work and what we are doing.

I opened the file she had given me but I could not read it and I asked, What is it about?

About what happened in the war.

She took me to a map on the wall with many coloured flags marking all the regions where she had interviewed women. I did not know what I was looking at, and she said, I am building cases to prosecute.

I asked, What happened to them?

She said, What happens to women in war.

Outside the office door, two volunteers were laughing.

I wondered, What did each flag mean? How many women?

Edina said, Let's go for coffee.

I suggested the Zlatna Ribica. I liked the decorations, the manual typewriters with broken keys and hand-coloured orientalist Victorian prints in small frames. I told her that in Paris I had been employed in a shop where I water-coloured and framed black-and-white prints cut from books, repainting history to decorate sitting rooms. And I wanted to see the foreign money under glass on the tables and the crystal and silver and costume jewellery hanging from hooks and the mirrors in ornate frames.

She said, There will be trials in The Hague.

For the women too?

They say, yes. It is a shock every time a woman tells. Do you know what it is to have blank sleep?

I did not.

Let's play chess, she said.

In that first game she stopped me from castling and my king never found safe haven. The game was over in twenty moves. She was good and I had not played since I had lived at home, when my father was still alive and we set up the board on Sunday afternoons. I can still feel the slant of warm sunshine over his companionable play. Edina played aggressively and with great concentration, controlled the centre of the board. My style was dishevelled, and I upset the expected order because I had not studied the game. Still, I enjoyed playing with her and we began to know each other without words, through our wooden men and their movement through each other's territory. At one point I did something unconventional—irrational, really—and she studied it and realized I had no plan and she glanced up through her hair at me and said, You are only a wood pusher. I said, No, not at all, and near the end of the game, when it became clear she would win, she joked, You are poisoning me with these bad moves. In this world she was sovereign and good-humoured and at the end of our game she swept all the pieces into a box and then she relaxed.

What is your daughter's name? she asked.

Biddy.

How old?

Almost twelve.

Does she like school?

Yes. Science.

Who takes care of her when you are away?

My mother.

She told me that her mother too had helped with her daughter, Merima, after the war. She said that Merima had to learn a new language and was now at university. She said that her daughter would never come back, so she had to travel to see her in Vienna. She said, I missed a lot with her because of the war.

The golden light at the bar flickered with a power surge.

I asked, What happened to your husband?

Gone.

In the thin light her skin looked eaten.

She asked, Isn't Kosmos waiting for you?

Probably.

Edina lit another cigarette and said, Let's play again. Timed game. You must try this time.

I asked, What does *zlatna ribica* mean?

She set up her pieces and gave me white and said, It means goldfish. If you catch a goldfish you get three wishes. Maybe you will catch one and wish for help with your game.

I had to smile. I opened with e4, and she moved so quickly I had difficulty following and I had to take time to consider, to try to understand what was happening. She was crushing me, and quickly she took my second bishop and I was working hard but she could see an amateur's patterns ahead. I struggled to keep up. She said, Tomorrow I meet for the first time lawyers from The Hague. They want to build a case. They will look at my files. Would you like to come?

KOSMOS WAS ASLEEP on my bed, eyebrows up. In Paris I had often found him waiting for me like this in my room. His body, at rest, vulnerable.

He stirred, said, Come to bed?

His touch was careful, fingers turning the pages of an old and brittle photo album. Was this what he remembered? Was this? What had happened since we had held each other, untroubled strangers, in Paris? I think we were trying to figure out if we loved each other. Our bodies did. With touch we asked each other, What happened to you? A baby. What happened to you? A war. Who are you now? How long is love? How short?

Love out of time. Eleven years apart. We told each other what had happened since the day he disappeared. He wanted to know everything about Biddy. He wanted to know how I lived, about my writing, about why I had to come to Sarajevo. He told me about his job managing a small theatre. There was little work in his city and less for artists. I asked if he had had girlfriends, perhaps a wife. He laughed and said marriage was not in his destiny, and I felt his mask slipping and I wanted to be alone with him for a thousand days so we could tell each other everything. I thought, We cannot tell eleven years in a single day.

We fell asleep again and when my alarm went off after only a few hours he said, You are going to her meeting. She told me she would ask you.

Does she tell you everything?

Mostly, he said.

He reached for my hand, pretending to pull me back to bed, and he said, I like you here.

I said, So do I. But I won't stay long. I need to get back to our daughter.

He got up and pulled on his pants and T-shirt and drove me through the awakening streets to Edina's office and I saw a small group of well-dressed women carrying bags and briefcases.

Kosmos said, There they are. I'll see you later.

I said, Thanks for the ride.

Paris

I MET KOSMOS in a bookshop called Shakespeare and Company at 37 rue de la Bûcherie. I was twenty years old. The bookshop's small rooms were piled to the ceilings with books, and above an inner doorway I read the hand-painted words *BE NOT INHOSPITABLE TO STRANGERS LEST THEY BE ANGELS IN DISGUISE.* George Whitman, owner of the shop, wore a paisley jacket. He was slender of face with piercing eyes and white hair. He sat reading and smoking.

I asked George, Can I stay here?

He reached under the counter and handed me a long metal file and pointed to a bicycle locked with a rusty chain to a post outside. The day was hot, sun bouncing off the yellow buildings. I filed and looked across the river at the great medieval church with its carved mandalas and gargoyles. George left and hours later returned with more books wrapped in a newspaper. At twilight I finally heard the exquisite *click* of a rusted chain. I unwrapped it from around the bicycle, gathered it over my arm and took it back into the shop where George sat on his perch surveying the world like a wandering falcon. I handed him his file and the old chain, and he looked at me as if he were trying to know something.

You can stay as long as you like, he said.

Where do I sleep?

He did not answer, only glanced upward as if at a ghost passing before returning to his book.

I stepped on a low stair on which was written *LIVE FOR HUMANITY* and pulled the shop around me like a worn quilt; tatty armchairs, kitchen on the second floor, narrow staircases where people fell down drunk, doorways crowded with spirits. Stacks of books. On the walls were black-and-white photos of writers whose androgynous faces showed the torment and wonder of a life conjured by words.

I was awoken that night by fireworks in the sky over Notre-Dame, yellow and red and blue explosions of metal salts. In the bookshop refuge I read, and with a borrowed black pen I wrote on my backpack a twice-translated line by Basho—*possessed by the spirits of wanderlust*—and wondered what it looked like and sounded like in Japanese. I felt agreeably alone in the world, walking on cobblestone during the days and falling asleep among other wanderers at night.

I WENT TO Paris because I wanted to be far from home. I was finished university and writing articles for *Canadian Forum* and waiting tables and trying to figure out how I wanted to live. Then, one night, my father was dancing with my mother and in the middle of "Sally Goodin" the electrical signals in his heart failed and he lost all feeling in his toes and fingers and his occipital cortex went black. Her hand was the last thing he must have seen as his long legs buckled. He crumpled toward the floor and in three minutes, the time it takes to boil an egg, my father was dead. I went home to be with Mam. She sat day after day at the kitchen table and said there was nothing to do but to accept the deaths of the men she loved. We buried his ashes together and my brother went back to work and Mam said she was going to learn to fly.

My brother was lucky. He was absorbed in his first year practising law. But I had no heart for my former life. I felt a new urgency to be in the world and I did not want to stay home with Mam. She told me secrets as if she had taken off a heavy coat in her grief. She drove to the airfield in the morning and when she came home she put on a messy half-open kimono and sat at the table and talked.

She said, I have ridden in an ambulance with my husband's dead body. I have organized a cremation with a mortician who forced me to sit near him so he could tell me his troubles. I planned the words, ashes to ashes and *joyful, joyful, melt the clouds of sin and sadness, drive the dark of doubt away*. I am the widow who has buried her husband's ashes in a velvet bag. I have mailed death certificates to strangers and paid death taxes and organized papers for banks and government departments. This is the business of death.

I wanted to hear my father's gentle voice again. I wanted life not to have stopped.

She said, The men I love die.

I did not want her to be complicated in this way. I did not want her lostness or her sorrow.

Why, I asked, do you keep talking about *men*?

When I was still a teenager, she said, I went to do war work. There was no money for more school for me. I was sent to Fifteen Wing, the air force base on the prairie, and I learned to repair fuselages. I worked underneath on my back on a dolly with a long, curved needle. I liked the other girls and we played softball at night and we had purpose and we were away from home. I really wanted to learn to fly and I used to help the young pilots study and I learned everything they did. I could have been a girl pilot but that was for rich girls.

Mam poured us another cup of tea. We did not drink it. She looked out the kitchen window toward a cardinal's *cheer-eet, cheer-eet*, and then she said, At Fifteen Wing, when you fixed a plane you had to test-fly in it to prove you hadn't sabotaged it. A pilot called Jack Eastmund liked me and came looking for me and he said, Where is Jean? I don't think she's been up in that plane she fixed.

We fell in love on that first flight and I let him touch my hand as he flew us over the prairie. We had five months on the base together before he shipped out to France. I was afraid of getting pregnant and somehow I managed not to. I don't know how and I was always worried about that. We planned to open a flight school together after the war, and he wrote to his parents about me, and I told the girls I was going to finally learn to fly and I was in love. It was war and it was a romantic time. But then the thousand-bomber raids. He wrote about flying four hundred knots and the wings are supposed to drop off at three hundred but they didn't. He said he could change directions in six seconds. Mostly he wrote how much he loved me and he kept telling me to hang on, he was coming home. I wrote, Be careful, come back to me, I'm planning our flight school, I'm thinking of you. But on a fogged-in night, my gentle, handsome Jack Eastmund never came back.

This was Mam's life before my father. Before me. I knew nothing about her.

She said, I burned Jack's letters yesterday. But I want someone to know about him. He is buried in Choloy.

And she looked away.

Families sometimes tell each other things so shocking that no one knows what to say. So no one says anything. As if the words had not been spoken.

My father was gone, his loving eyes that were always interested in me, his gentle, sheepish smile. But she was talking about another man.

She said to the window, not to me, I wonder what life would have been like if I'd got pregnant with him.

I thought, People break their secrets inside you, whether you can bear to hold the pieces or not.

I said to Mam, When I go to France I will go to see where Jack Eastmund is buried.

You're going to France?

Yes, Paris.

She considered this, decided something and said, No need to see where Jack Eastmund is buried. You know where your father is buried.

She stood, dumped our full teacups in the sink, said, I have weeding to do.

She could rest. Jack Eastmund was now buried in me.

When she came back from the garden she went to the kitchen sink and washed her large hands, her cuticles dirt-stained and torn. She had picked three large ripe tomatoes and they shone red on the counter in the afternoon light. She rinsed off the dirt but left the green stems. I love the smell of tomatoes on the vine, earth and sun and taut skins. She looked into my eyes and she said, You should go. I will miss you but you should go.

I only wanted to get away from her, from her ice pit of sadness, from absence no one but the dead could fill. I could not bring myself to be tender with her and I could not even say, I will miss you too.

And in this chaotic grief, a startling idea stood naked and waiting: *why not be free.*

—

JACK EASTMUND HAD been transferred to Squadron 420, the Snowy Owls, who were part of Operation Gomorrah and the firestorm on Hamburg. He flew the planes that dropped thousands of aluminum foil strips designed to interfere with radar signals and to blind the enemy defences. More planes followed and attacked with a wave of incendiaries and explosives that turned the streets into tunnels of fire. Asphalt melted and trapped the feet of people trying to run away. People wrapped in blankets in buildings turned to ash, like tissues dropped into a campfire. Karla Vogel's family's apartment was in Heussweg, above her father's shop. The fires exploded windows and in minutes gutted whole streets of her neighbourhood. The firestorm sounded like a pipe organ with all the keys pressed at once. Ten thousand tons of bombs dropped in seven hellish summer days. Karla's mother woke her up in their borrowed farmhouse in the countryside far from the city and said, We got out in time.

Inside his plane Jack Eastmund felt the heat of a city aflame. He had never felt such a thing in the cool sky. He wanted to think about a girl. He wanted to think about love and the quiet prairie where he grew up. But all he could see was fire.

I FOUND A job in an antiques shop in the Marais cutting prints from old books and hand-colouring and framing them to sell. It was pleasant work that required a steady hand but no thought at all, and when we took breaks the owner brought us fresh baguettes and chocolate. I loved to walk among the synagogues and Asian shops in that quartier, breathing in the earthy tea smell of the plane trees and looking at French books in Les Mots à la Bouche. The antiques shop owner paid me under the table, and as soon as I had enough money I moved out of Shakespeare's to a *chambre de bonne* on the sixth floor of an old apartment building on the rue des Écoles. My new room measured a handful of square metres, was unheated, had a single bed, a cold-water sink, a small table and chair. From my tiny balcony I could see the Seine and Notre-Dame and I was happy. Down the unlit hall was a squat toilet shared with the other maids' rooms on our floor. If I ran up the six floors I could make it to the top before the timed lights went out.

One night one of my neighbours was standing by my door with a carton of cigarettes and a bottle of wine. I had seen him in the hall, always alone. Perhaps he suffered as I did from Parisian coldness toward people like us. He said his name was Rafiq and I told him mine was Gota. I was afraid and told him in my accented French that he could not come in, that I slept only with women, and he laughed and said that he did not believe me and do not worry he would not hurt me and then we both went back into our separate rooms.

Soon after, I saw him coming and going with a new girl-friend called Lulu and we became friends. *Bonjour, Rafiq. Salut, Lulu.* They nicknamed me Goat in French, which sounded funny, and they called across the street, *Ciao, Chèvre!* Sometimes we sat together in the café downstairs and talked about movies and books.

I had a camping stove to boil water and I drank instant coffee standing on my balcony looking over the city. I enrolled at the Sorbonne, which was very cheap, and with my student card I could go to museums and galleries and eat in cheap student restaurants and sit in libraries. I was especially fond of a small library on the top floor of a building on boulevard Saint-Michel with a window looking toward Versailles. In Paris I often perched in places overlooking the city, a temporary roost in this life I had created out of flight and migration.

KOSMOS WAS IN the kitchen at Shakespeare's with other travellers, pouring damson plum spirits, telling stories and swearing. I liked how his long hair fell across his eyes and the way he spoke English as if it were coming from a grave in his throat. He wore a black jacket over a dark green T-shirt. He was performing, joking about an Olympic skating routine in his hometown of Sarajevo, said that the repeating-like-a-broken-washing-machine-*Bolero* was inferior to Ravel's melancholy *Don Quichotte à Dulcinée*. I left the doorway to sit down at the end of the table facing him. He lifted an empty glass toward me, eyebrows raised, poured me a half tumbler. I took it and drank it all. He lifted his own glass and drank, his eyes not leaving mine.

In truth, I think *Bolero* is a finer piece of music, I said.

Not at all, said Kosmos.

J'étoilerais le vent qui passe, I said.

We were showing off because we wanted each other, our bodies two strings on a spike lute. Soon we were walking alone along the Seine. By midnight he was telling me about the play he wanted to write and had I read this famous book, *The Bridge on the Drina*, in which the main character was a silent bridge? He was wound up and telling me about his theatre group, Mess, and that his play would be about lovers on bridges in his country, where they met and joined their souls or jumped off, everyone trying to be somewhere else no matter where they were born centuries before and would it not be a marvellous play?

He spoke with the unusual archaisms of someone who has learned English from old books. He said that his grandparents had a farm near the Drina, the home of his deepest memories.

I knew nothing of the places and things and languages he spoke of, but I liked the timbre of his voice and the light in his eyes. I liked his smell.

He said, My play will begin with a famous story from Andrić about a bridge built by Rade the Mason. Every night someone was destroying the day's work. To stop the destruction, Rade ordered his men to find Christian twins, a boy and girl named Stoja and Ostoja, and to wall them into the bridge's middle pier. His men stole the babies from a distant place, and their wailing mother followed them all the way to the bridge. Rade felt pity so he entombed them alive but left an opening for their mother to nurse them. To this day people collect the thin white stream that mysteriously appears from the stone.

Kosmos paused to see if I was enjoying his story.

I said, This is pity?

THAT FIRST NIGHT together sitting by the Seine, Kosmos told me he would take me to see the kapia on his favourite bridge, a stone sofa above rushing water where people came to trade and talk near the coffee-merchant with his charcoal brazier and copper pots and small cups. Kosmos said, Everyone meets on the bridge.

Then he counted on his fingers until he ran out and started again—Turks, Serbs, Roma, Bosnians, Moslems and Roman Catholics and Orthodox Christians and Sephardic Jews, people who speak Ekavian and Turcizmi and Serbo-Croatian and

German and Ladino and Arabic and Persian. He dropped his hands and touched my hand for the first time and my blood and breath quickened with this first touch of flesh. He smelled perfect, mountain-grass-sweet skin and salt-ocean sweat.

I asked, Is Kosmos your last name or first?

It is my only name, he said. In my left-nut-is-dancing-messed-up country, a person gets killed for a name. I do not tell any other name.

He put his arm around me, warmth against the quay's cold stone.

I said, Soon the sun will rise just above Notre-Dame.

He asked, Do you think a bridge built by slaves can be the place for a love story?

Preserve me from the violent . . . continually are they gathered together for war.

I said, There must be atonement, apology, purification. Why was your bridge built by slaves?

Stories ran thick as spawning salmon in Kosmos's head. Pulling me closer, he told me about the slave Radisav who destroyed the bridge-building work from a simple raft in the darkness every night. When he was caught, he was wrapped in hot, thick metal chains and his toenails were torn from his feet with pincers. The leader Abidaga asked him, What makes you destroy the bridge?

Radisav said, It is the devil.

Abidaga asked, What devil?

Radisav answered, The same devil who makes you enslave us to build it.

Then intolerable things happened to him. They impaled him through spread legs all the way up under his spine so the wooden rod touched no organs, no heart, no lungs, and did not kill him. He was kept alive gushing blood from the coccyx and the top of the spine and he was hung skewered over the river. The children who usually played by the river watched the torture and absorbed fear through their skin like frogs. All the town was silent but for his screams.

And when the terror finally ended, the bridge was built with no further resistance.

Kosmos said, Why do I tell you such terrible stories when I want to kiss you? I come from a place of endless torment and war.

I thought, Do not fall in love with him.

I said, I can see your bridge arched over a stage, actors jumping from it and lifting themselves up on pulleys. I can see lovers meeting on the stone couches.

Then I stood and pulled him up and I said, My home also is a land of many languages—Huron, Algonquin, Iroquois and Montagnais. The Europeans wrote letters back home in French and Italian and Latin. In my home too was war and torture over territory, and the destruction of peoples for land, for ideas, for religion. Why should anyone claim the freedom of another?

The pulsing blood. I had to step away from him and so I pretended to be an old explorer and I raised my hand over the Seine and said, I claim this place under the authority of the Doctrine of Discovery.

I intoned to the cathedral, You gargoyles, especially you bored one resting on your elbows, you indigenous-creatures-who-are-not-human, your land is *terra nullius* and I claim it.

Kosmos was laughing at me and he understood little of what I was playing at, as I had understood little of his bridges. We are each born of particular violence on this blue and green planet in

33

a dark and lifeless universe, and rather than be here together in awe, we war with each other.

I was not thinking about any of this that first night with Kosmos. No matter how many violent stories we told each other to pass the dark hours, we were really only thinking about making love together. All that first night until dawn we talked. The truly devastating things had not yet happened.

The yellow buildings behind Notre-Dame turned golden in the early pale sun, which shone first red and then white in the sky.

I told him I had a room nearby and Kosmos said he would walk back with me. On the rue des Écoles I unlocked the tall wooden door with my heavy key. I told him to follow me up the stairs quickly because I did not want my old French landlady, whose birds I sometimes took care of, to hear us, and neither did I want to disturb Rafiq and the others on my floor who were sure to be still asleep.

HE WENT OUT on my tiny balcony and said, You can see the whole city. I pulled from under the bed my small collection of cassette tapes and I put on the Vienna Symphony Orchestra playing *Bolero*. That first time was in the long dawn and I remember him above me and the sounds outside of the awakening street and our eyes asking, accepting, and I remember how I opened to him and how slow he was. Then we fell asleep and woke and made love again, this time with more hunger and more wild. He slept with his eyebrows raised as if in endless wonder at the world. When I woke again in the early afternoon he was sitting naked over a sheet of paper at my little table.

What are you writing?

I am writing you a goodbye letter, but I don't want to.

You are in love with someone else.

He crumpled up the paper, said, Does my face really tell every fucked-up secret?

I said, Your language sounds terrible in English.

English is thin, he said. In my language we are creative with our words.

Tell me about her.

Don't ask this, it is fucked up. Do not want to know.

Tell me.

He stood, looked out the window. Nothing to tell, he said. She is married. I met her at an art show with her husband in Sarajevo and then I left.

What is her name?

I cannot talk about her when I just made love with you.

I said, At least it is not cowardly like leaving a letter.

I pulled the sheet up and he unfolded the crumpled letter and refolded it into an airplane and went naked onto the balcony and threw it to glide down into the street. He turned and said, Edina.

He was right. Her name was now between us like a punch. But he also looked outrageous without clothes outside on my balcony, and his buttocks were muscular and round above strong thighs. Confusing feelings feel normal when you are young. I was laughing at him and I said, Come inside. You are going to get me in trouble going out naked and you will get me kicked out of this room and it is difficult to find a room in Paris.

I wanted to know him. I wanted to show off for him and I wanted him to watch me. He let me bring him back to my bed and this time we came together, and then he got up and I watched him get dressed. We had so much energy. I knew now he would leave and I said, *Va te faire foutre.*

He laughed and said, You see, you swear too and English is not good enough for you either.

I said, You're like a bird that flew, see you on the avenue.

He said, Can I come here again?

I listened to his steps echo down the six flights of stairs and when I heard them on the tiles of the foyer at the bottom, I went out on the balcony naked and wrapped in the sheet from my bed. He turned to look up at my window and he waved and I could still feel his hands on my back. Already I loved him, and I had to drop the sheet to wave goodbye.

MY FATHER KEPT a real human skull high on our bookshelf. He used it to teach dental students, and my brother and I liked to play cannibals with it. We put it on a piano-stool altar. We were imitating a Looney Tunes cartoon of a toaster salesman who was sentenced to be a husband to the Queen of the Cannibals. My brother and I found this very funny, especially how the salesman jumped into the pot of boiling water so he would not have to get married. One day my father caught us and he came in and gently reached into the middle of our game and took the skull from us and said, That belonged to a living human being.

He was generally mild with us so when he took the skull that day it marked me. My brother does not remember the incident. What is powerful for one is not even remembered by another.

—

KOSMOS HAD A motorcycle with a sidecar and every night we rode through the empty Paris streets. We made love. Went out again. Were ravenous. Ate cheap gyros on the street. In the daytime I worked at the print shop and wrote at lunch and he went to the library at Georges Pompidou and worked on his play about bridges. I sent an article about Parisian bookshops to *Canadian Forum* and the editor wrote back and asked me to send more stories. I was happy. Kosmos earned a little money in the late afternoons washing dishes in an Arab café and sometimes he brought us leftover couscous. We often went to look at the stained glass windows of La Sainte-Chapelle, dark zaffre and gold starred patterns, ruby and indigo. Under those windows when no priest was looking we embraced and he said, We will always be once-in-blue-moons.

I said, Why? We can be more.

He said, But I cannot.

Perhaps you could.

Hope is irrational but we endlessly hope.

Later, on my narrow single bed, he pulled me closer and said, Do not fall in love with me.

Too late.

Always he kept a little distance. Then blew on the ember. We drove out of town and explored the countryside, ate crêpes in Beaugency, drank coffee in Versailles, went to a medieval street fair with jugglers and spice merchants in Vincennes. He told me he would one day leave. But I did not listen. My love was uninvited fever, reason past care, consuming, and I was helpless in it. I knew I would never have this again and I wanted all of it, tinder and wild fire.

My room had no doorbell. He would park his motorbike under my window and honk for me. One night he must have been drunk because he wouldn't stop honking when I did not wake up and someone from the second-floor apartment leaned out the window and dropped a bottle of milk on his helmet. I knew nothing of any of this until I left for work and saw broken glass on the sidewalk. In the afternoon I went to look for him at Shakespeare's to tell him my news. He wasn't downstairs so I ran up the Hafiz staircase, a few words on each step—*I wish . . . I could show you . . . when you are . . . lonely or . . . in darkness . . . the astonishing . . . light . . . of your own . . . being*—and there he was at the top, reading, I thought, waiting for me. I moved his book and sat on his lap and he told me about the milk bottle. He said he would have been killed if he had not been wearing a helmet.

I said, Let's go for a ride. I have something to tell you.

But he said, I can't. I am going to the airport.

Where?

He said, I have to go.

I was so surprised I could not speak.

He said, Do not be angry. I will write soon.

The subharmonics of lies.

I said, Write? I don't want paper.

Please, he said. He put his arms around me. From the first time he had warned me.

His hair fell over his left eye.

He said, I have to memorize your face. I want you to remember how I almost died for you on my last night in Paris.

Ta gueule, I said.

He liked my bad language and I was studying his rueful smile and he said, I have to go before I change my mind. I cannot stay here. I don't want to hurt you. I do not love as you do.

And then he let me go.

The rude severing, never, never again trust the body's desire.

He walked down the steps ... *being* ... *of your own* ... *light* ... *the astonishing* ... and I thought, What am I going to do now? And he disappeared through the door.

I looked into the empty space where he had been. I thought, I will love you even to death, even while my ashes are being tossed into the wind and there is nothing left of me, still I will love you.

I sat on the floor with a book that I did not read and when I went downstairs a little later, George was sitting out front smoking, his birdcage on the sidewalk beside him. He tipped the silver case in which he kept his hand-rolled cigarettes toward me and I took one and sat down beside him. The budgies were making a racket.

What's wrong with them? I asked. The soothing nicotine. The wretched flavour. The irritating birds.

There is a new one in there, he said. They're claiming their territory, I imagine.

Tssssk. Tsssssk.

Small territory, I said.

Always is, said George.

We watched them and watched the darkness over Notre-Dame.

He left, I said.

Who?

You know, Kosmos. Didn't you see him?

I don't keep track of the tumbleweeds, said George. Where did he go?

He would not say.

Your Ottoman lover, said George.

I might die, I said.

George rubbed the end of his cigarette between his fingers.

Love's not Time's fool, he said, *Love alters not with his brief hours and weeks, but bears it out even to the edge of doom.*

That's no answer, I said.

Poetry is always an answer, said George.

I WROTE LETTERS to Mam about working in the shop and about Shakespeare's and I sent her the short pieces I was mailing to *Canadian Forum,* Notes from a Flaneuse in Paris, though I did not attach much importance to them. Mam's letters described the garden and the election and what she was reading. The night she got her glider licence she wrote on the outside of the envelope, *Celebrate!* Loneliness seeped through her familiar large-looped handwriting. I pictured her sitting at the kitchen table with her writing box open, choosing a card and lifting her pen. She wrote that now she was going to train to fly cross-country. She described the sensation of a hot thermal, the rushing sound and rising in the air. In another letter she wrote that she wanted soon to sell the old family house and move somewhere else and at the very end of the page she wrote that a man had asked her on a date. She ran out of paper so she turned the page sideways and wrote up the margins and around the top as if writing sideways was a better way to tell certain stories. *It is flattering,* she wrote, *but my word, he just wants to sit around—our first date we went to a movie and the next time he wanted to come to my house to dinner—I don't want to take care of any more men—or anyone—the garden is almost done now—I'm drying mint this year—love, Mam.* And she put a mint leaf in the envelope.

—

KOSMOS SENT ME postcards but there was never a return address or a surname. The first card was a photo of a wall and barbed wire and he wrote, *Thinking of you in Berlin.* Next was an antique card from a dervish house, *I am thinking about bridges and you and I am writing my play.* And then a card with a picture of the ocean from Mljet Island on which he wrote, *If you were here, Calypso, we could stay seven years.*

I wanted to write, *Go home to Penelope.*

The last card I ever received from him was a Henry Payne painting of men choosing between red or white roses. On the other side, *I must decide to go home or not, thinking of you.* It was mailed from London. The card was an advertisement for a play at the National Theatre and I wondered if he had found work there. I mailed a letter to Kosmos, c/o The National Theatre, London, England, to tell him my news, but I received no answer.

I left Paris forever a few months after he did. I could not survive living in a cold-water walk-up and working under the table in a print shop.

I could not imagine doing what I was going to do alone.

I gave my landlady a forwarding address, but the old woman never forwarded anything. If cards came, she probably used them to line the bottom of her birdcage.

Mam met me at the airport. When the thick glass doors opened into the world I came from, my young city of immigrants and refugees and people born on the land, I felt destroyed. I did not want to be here and I did not want to be in Paris. There Mam stood alone, where she and my father used to be. Her curly hair was pulled up at the back of her skull in a way that made her high cheekbones pretty. She held her arms open to pull me close and I could see she had thrived in the year we had not seen each other. She was holding me in the crowd at arrivals and she smelled like our old home.

She said, I missed you.

I'm pregnant, I said.

Toronto, Sarajevo

I WANTED TO keep my baby. I look back now and it seems simple but it did not feel simple then. How would I support a child and how would I work? How would it be for her with no father? Who would be her family?

But there was this other feeling that I had few words for. It was a feeling of *I can do what I want*. It was in the air. Women were speaking. Shedding old shames. Working as bus drivers. As judges. As radio hosts. Keeping their babies. People said things like, *I don't like a woman's voice on the radio*, or, *Women are too emotional for boardrooms*. But women kept doing things anyway. I watched people condemn my rounding stomach and look for a ring on my finger. I told Mam about this and she said, It's none of their beeswax.

I had to laugh. I could not remember her being defiant in this way.

I said, So the wedding part does not bother you.

She said, Don't let them criticize you. Live your life.

I wish I could give this fierceness to all young women.

Mam showed me an enormous old family Bible. On the *Births, Deaths and Marriages* pages, someone had scrawled after my great-great-great-grandmother Bridget-Margaret Muireb's name, *Biddy*. She was nine years old when she left Ireland during a famine. What did she do? Who took care of her? She had got pregnant by a soldier back from the Crimean War and she died in childbirth at sixteen. Hunger. Child pregnancy. Death. This tale of her life was written on a piece of vellum paper in fountain pen ink and tucked between the pages of Genesis by the same anonymous and neat hand that had written her nickname on the family tree.

Mam said, Our whole line comes from that girl.

FOR A WHILE I tried to forget about Kosmos. I got a job with an airline magazine, easy, disposable writing, flip it open, wait for the flight to be over. The editor was Jacques Payac, a former newspaperman and a war correspondent. He had been hit by shrapnel and his left leg was amputated above the knee so he took a desk job. At the interview I told him about my life in Paris, about living in a bookshop and working at the print shop on the Place des Vosges. I showed him a couple of my pieces, one about releasing ortolans from their fate as a delicacy to be eaten under napkins. He laughed at that one and hired me for features and said, I don't have much money. But you'll have fun. Short trips. Write for tourists. Find interesting angles.

I said, Sounds good. Thank you.

He rose crookedly, righted himself, extended his hand to shake mine and said, Start tomorrow.

I picked up my bag and when I was partway through the door he asked, By the way, are you pregnant?

I said, See you in the morning.

He said, All right.

I thought, Even if I do not get to keep this job I will be friends with this man.

This began a busy time of travel and the best job I could have hoped for. I went for a week to Egypt to write about the pyramids because of a new direct Cairo route. While I was there I did not stay in the airline hotel but I lived with an old woman in the tombs in the City of the Dead below the Mokattam hills. I wrote about that. I went to Angkor Wat because of new flights to Asia and I travelled to the pepper fields to see the hidden HIV villages. Back at home I travelled on a float plane up the Labrador coast to cover some American hunting lodges and I stopped at Hebron where all but four people died of the 1918 flu. The survivors chopped holes in the ice and weighted the corpses with rocks in the freezing water until they could bury them in the spring.

Everywhere I went I wrote two pieces, one a travel piece for the magazine and one about what I really saw. Jacques called me *young man* and he was gnarly and pragmatic and occasionally he asked me to verify facts, distances, prices, locations. He said, You're cheaper than a bunch of freelancers and you're fast. I just have to keep making up pseudonyms for you.

I wrote a piece about walls engraved with the names of the dead. Names cut into marble and granite, carved into wood and stone, nailed onto trees and doorways and fences. Even on the moon they left a plaque to dead astronauts. Walls and borders are the natural habitat of ghosts. I do not invite ghosts in but I do not close myself to them either. I hear their voices like bird-call in the dark. They are perceptible through stone and brick and plaster. I think sometimes ghosts surprise even themselves. They have things to tell us. If we can hear, they are everywhere.

One day Jacques called me into his office and I saw the stack of my what-I-really-saw pieces and he tapped his finger on them and said, Why so much death and disease, young man? What am I supposed to do with these?

I don't know. Publish them.

WHEN I GOT too pregnant to fly, Jacques taught me copy editing and layout. I had travelled so much and written so fast that we had a year's worth of material anyway. He gave me a travel gadgets section at the back to write—portable luggage weigh scales and ostrich feather pillows and rabbit-ear corkscrews. The advertisers loved it and I marvelled at human ingenuity put to no purpose at all. I liked to sit late at the office with Jacques while he rolled cigarettes and smoked. Sometimes I talked to him about journalists like Daniel Defoe and I.F. Stone who put together stories from what was around them, from public domain records and industry reports.

He said, You just say that because you're chained to home like I am. What are you hanging around with an old guy for?

I said, You're the only writer I know.

Lord help you then, and he leaned back in his chair and put his good leg up on the desk.

I said, You know what they have in Belfast?

To make him laugh I told him about the loos that rise out of the sidewalks after dark, and I said I wanted to do a feature on international *uritrottoirs*. He asked why I hadn't thought of being a real reporter.

I said, Someday.

Oh, he said, the kid.

Jacques smoked deep into his lungs and held his hand-rolled cigarettes with his thumb and forefinger from above and mostly did not talk when he smoked, as if smoking and talking were separate activities.

He blew rings. Finally he said, Why not rewrite some of your ghost stories. Five hundred words.

I said, They're not ghost stories.

He said, I can publish them under a different byline, maybe Joe de Pone.

Will Joe de Pone get paid?

Joe's expenses are the same as yours. I can find fifty cents a word.

It sounds like my work just doubled.

Suit yourself.

I said, I want it.

Jacques buried my Joe de Pone column at the back of the magazine between the ads. Once I was at a party and someone said that my colleague de Pone must be a strange man to write about such obscure, sad things.

I said, He's a good guy. Not much different from you or me.

I BOUGHT A house on Sibelius Park with money my father left, his last gift. My house was made of brick and it was close to a school, with a front porch and a tree, a good place to raise a child.

The day I moved in, Mam came over with a cardboard box. She said, House-warming present. It's a cast of my grandmother's face. My grandfather made it.

Inside the box was a smooth white plaster cast. The face had high cheekbones and was delicate and heart shaped. The eyelids over the eyes seemed large under the small forehead. I imagined the teenaged girl lying still while her older fiancé made a cast of her face. Did she think it was romantic that he wanted to preserve her image in this way? Was she flattered that he wanted a copy of her face? How did she breathe while the older man hovered over her, waiting for the plaster to dry?

Mam said, My grandfather was a strange, violent man. I was afraid of him. We stayed out of his way. I don't know what he did except church three times on the Sabbath and his taxidermy in the back porch. You couldn't even iron a shirt on a Sunday.

Mam traced her finger over the small nose, the firm chin. She said, But everyone loved my grandmother. Her name was Minnie Mae.

I said, Let's hang her in the living room.

Mam said, I'm selling the big house. I don't need it anymore. I was thinking I could move to that low-rise across the park from you and help with the baby. But if you don't want this, I'll move out close to the airfield.

What about not wanting to take care of anyone?

You're not anyone, she said.

She offered me small delicacies during my pregnancy, vanilla from orchids and rosehip teas and daisy oil, and a recording of Prokofiev's *Romeo and Juliet* because I love the double bass.

She said, These are tender days, Gota.

WHILE I WAS having my baby and watching her grow, I did not know where Kosmos was. I was at home making a childhood for Biddy with birthdays and parks and slides and swings, flying with Mam and swimming in the lake, ice-skating and walking in the ravines. But other women were trying to take care of their children in wars. I saw them when I watched television.

The world watched. Did nothing. Edina was there. Edina was no longer a lawyer in a loving marriage, a woman who walked on a summer evening with her family. She was filthy and thirsty, hiding from soldiers in a mountain forest. She watched her father shot in front of her, saw her mother and her daughter dragged away by soldiers in heavy boots. She was locked up and raped day after day, beaten, starved and assaulted. No one was coming.

THE DISAPPEARING MINUTES of the newborn are water over a stone. When I walked with Biddy I had passing daydreams about turning a corner and seeing Kosmos. I was sometimes lonely in the sleepless first months, when my arms ached and my breasts were full, when I lived in minutes and not hours. I used to walk with her to Mam's apartment across the park or to Jacques Payac's office on Bathurst Street or to the mothers' groups where I listened to young women complaining about their partners not helping enough and about feeling sticky and exhausted and not wanting to be touched. This was strange to me. I wanted to be touched. I told them I freelanced, that Mam came every day, that, in fact, I did not get tired of her help. She had a knack with babies, knew how to create calm. Sometimes when I was with her and the baby I felt a strange déjà vu, and I wondered if I were remembering my own baby time. Biddy must have felt it too because she was settled and curious and watched everything, sovereign over our tiny world. She was easy to soothe and distract. Sometimes late at night after she was asleep, Mam walked across the park. If I was reading or writing she did not come in, only said, Hello, just out for a walk.

But other times she sat with me on the porch for a while.

Are you lonely? she would ask.

I don't have time to be lonely. You?

She said, Not really.

Do you miss being married?

I could not bear to ask her if she missed my father.

We listened to the cry of a nightjar in the park, to the city's low thrum.

She said, The happiest years were when you and your brother were young. The happiness did diminish with time. We shared less that was new and more that was habit. But we kept trying. Started dancing.

Why did you get married?

I wanted children. After the war, people were glad to be alive. I lost my first love and I wanted to get on with life. But I wonder now why I thought my autonomy was worth less than his.

I had to remind myself that she was not betraying my father. She was only telling her own story.

She said, They told women to make room for the men, to give up their jobs for the men coming home. We thought it was the right thing. It was good for your father.

She looked into the darkness and said, At least young women don't have to get stuck in *that* image anymore.

But he was my beloved father. I had thought he was perfect.

I TOLD BIDDY about Kosmos as soon as she could talk and I showed her the only picture I had of the two of us, standing in front of his motorcycle near the Bastille. We called him Tata. I told her we would find him someday. I embellished the stories because what I had was thin. I could not tell her that we had spent as much time as we could in bed. I told her that we had lived in Paris together, that we had watched the sunrise over Notre-Dame and walked along the Seine. I told her he loved music, especially Ravel, and I had some recordings I could give her, and that he worked in theatre. She wanted more. I told her about my little room overlooking the rooftops and that he loved the balcony. I told her about the churches we visited and the Place des Vosges. I had to tell her more about Paris than about him because that was all I had. I told her someday we would visit his country. He loved the bridges in his country and on them were stone couches where people met each other suspended over fast-running mountain rivers and they listened to the water below.

She said, I would like to sit on a stone couch. And then she asked, Why don't we know where he is?

I don't know.

She had no father and no image of a father. She liked to look for faces in the bark of the tree where her swing hung. Mam showed her an abandoned nest hidden high in the leaves. When Biddy got older she liked to sit alone on the front porch and look at the stars. My curiosity about Biddy is fathomless. I felt sorry that she had no father like mine who loved me. She only had Mam and me. There is no perfect in a family.

A child is loaned to us and when the time is right the child is reclaimed by the world. And yet, mother and child are inside each other forever. A mother receives wisdom if she is willing to submit, if she is willing to love ferociously and then shake her child free.

I learned one kind of love from Mam and another from Biddy. I learned that I only felt right when my daughter and my mother felt right. We were wrapped around and through each other like the roots and branches of a wild banyan tree holding together an abandoned home for the compassionate god.

THE WAR WENT on and on. The world slowly roused itself like an old and weary dog. It stretched stiffly from its front legs up to the back, and then it shook, tried to take a step, to do something, to resist the thick urge for vengeance. Silence breaks people. There would be a negotiated end. They were writing indictments in The Hague and bringing in criminals and witnesses. My brother, with his retentive memory and a keen allegiance to fairness, had left practice to become a judge, and we often talked about the new court. He liked to visit on Sunday evenings to see Biddy. After she was in bed we watched the news and he asked, I wonder if your guy went back there.

I do too, I said. If they sentence people in The Hague, where will they incarcerate them?

My brother had visited prisons. When he started out as a judge he said he needed to feel what he would be condemning others to.

He answered, I suppose each country agrees to let them use their prisons.

Do you think they can really make an international understanding?

If everyone agrees. It's logical.

Law changes. Which means it is sometimes wrong.

You always say that, he said. It's imperfect. It's what we have.

We must not make a scarecrow of the law, I said.

What are you talking about?

It should change. When it stays the same, the birds use it as a perch.

Nice image, he said.

Not mine, I said. And spoken from a position of power.

I like quotes to start my judgments, he said. I might use that.

Je t'en prie, I said.

My brother's mind did not linger on a single strand. He liked to work on lots of threads at the same time. He was taking everything in. He watched baseball and read newspapers and looked through law books at the same time. He nodded toward the television and said, Those war criminals will not only be in prison but in exile.

After my brother left that night, I felt restless. I was tired of being alone. I wondered if I had fooled myself. *For I have sworn thee fair, and thought thee bright, who art as black as hell, as dark as night.* But I could no more deny my love than the sky can deny its stars. I could not make it make sense, but I was fine. Most of the time.

The next morning I was leaving for New York for three days and I worried aloud to Mam about leaving Biddy whenever I travelled for work and about feeling restless and needing to write about things I cared about.

Mam said, Gota, you've had it all.

Mam was rarely impatient and this stopped me. I said, I'm sorry.

She said, Work. Biddy's fine.

I said, I worry about being away.

Mam asked, Aren't I doing a good enough job?

I didn't mean that.

Biddy is doing what she is supposed to be doing.

What is that?
Learning not to need you.
But *I* still need *you*.
I know. I need you too. This is the strangeness of love.

EVERY NIGHT WE saw more news stories about massacres and about refugees struggling along roads toward borders and one night the camera rested on a woman holding a child's lifeless body. I could not say, Oh that is only something happening far away because of war. I felt those images in my skin. I could not say I did not know. To turn away is to accept. To remain silent is to accept. Now they were opening the borders, inviting us to the besieged city. What was I going to do? Write about corkscrews with rabbit ears?

Sarajevo

KOSMOS HAD DROPPED me at Edina's office to join her first meeting with Karla Vogel-Babić, the lead prosecutor from The Hague. Edina led us upstairs, unlocked a door into a main office, led us down a hallway to a waiting room, and then she unlocked a second door into her own office, a small room with a worn couch and two low chairs around a table, bookcases on three walls, a row of file cabinets on the fourth wall, no window. Edina moved behind her cluttered desk and gestured us to sit.

Karla greeted Edina in Croatian, then said in her brisk and formal English, I am German, and my husband is from Croatia. Before the war we went every year to visit his family. I grew up in Hamburg. My city was destroyed. I joined the court in The Hague when it opened. We are very pleased to meet you. I understand you are a lawyer.

Edina nodded.

Karla introduced their interpreter Lise Favre-Rastoder, Swiss-Montenegrin, a huge woman with a comfortable smile, and Sue Rupasinghe, American–Sri Lankan, her co-counsel.

Edina introduced me, Gota Dobson. A friend.

Karla said, We are grateful to you for allowing us to see your files in order to build this case. Our preliminary investigations are leading us to many women who now live abroad. The statements you have gathered are from women who live throughout the region? We need to put all this together and to strategize.

Edina nodded.

Karla said, You know this trial will not be easy for the witnesses.

I know.

Edina pointed to the file cabinets and said, I will not endanger even one woman. They have been through enough. At the beginning I myself struggled over whether to stay silent or to speak. But I could not accept the morality of staying silent.

She fleetingly covered her face with her hands.

It is not good, she said, to close yourself up and to lock things inside. But with this trial there will be much pain.

She came around from behind her desk and sat across from Lise.

Karla said, There will be emotional needs. We can make arrangements for counselling and childcare and time away from work. The women can travel with someone to support them. This case depends on the women.

Edina answered slowly, Some women's families do not know. Women ask me if I know what it is like to have sex with a husband when you don't want it? When he does not know what happened to you? When you feel only pain?

She straightened some files and said, Do not think you are different because you have not been in this war. You *can* imagine. You know the feeling of sex when you do not want it. Maybe you even know the physical torment. If you ask the women to tell their stories you must not barricade yourselves off as if you do not know.

Our only wisdom is our humility, I thought.

Edina said to Lise, When you interpret you must become the voice of the other.

Lise said, My best work is invisible.

Edina answered, But to me, you are not invisible.

There was a tap at the door and a woman came in with a tray of coffee. Edina said, I will need a photocopier, paper, ink.

She picked up the six files on her desk, handed them to Lise and said, Read these and I will come back in a little while. If the women tell these stories in court they will have to relive that time. It was terrible and many of them have spent years trying to forget.

Lise took the first file on her lap, and Sue and Karla shifted forward to take notes.

Outside her office Edina and I settled on a small couch in the sitting area.

I asked, What do you think?

She said, I have enough files for a thousand trials. Last night I did not sleep.

Without awareness she reached for my hand and held it. She said, At first I did not want to be involved in anything like this. I wanted to be hidden, alone.

I nodded.

She said, In the war, the hardest time was at the beginning when I understood that no one was coming. I have never lost that feeling. This is the first time anyone has come.

She looked down at her hand over mine, took it away as if she had not known it was there.

She said, I sleep in a net of nightmares. I cannot be silent but I do not want to speak.

Then she got up and went downstairs alone.

A FEW HOURS later, Karla and Sue and Lise stood when we came back to the office. The files were open on the table and the coffee was gone. I waited by the door looking at paper on every surface. The women's expressions were grave, lips pulled tight, arms close to their bodies.

Karla asked, How many?

Edina lifted her right palm to the walls of file cabinets in her office. She pointed out the open door to the bank of cabinets along the hall, colour-coded to match the flags on the map of the region.

Karla asked, Do people know?

Edina said, People do not want to know.

WITH OUR CHESS pieces we tricked and taunted, challenged and blocked, joked and teased. Through our strategies and missteps, we got to know each other. Edina liked to play and smoke cigarettes and talk at the same time. She did not have to concentrate as much as I did because she was very good. She had learned in a girls' chess club at school under an unusual teacher who was enthusiastic for both boys and girls to play. She played with three girls in three neighbouring villages by mail until her father complained that her chess postage would soon be more expensive than their groceries. A few times her girls' club demanded to play the boys and she liked to beat the boys. She told me her parents did not play well—only knew the moves—but they came to her tournaments in the same way they came to her school concerts, and afterwards they met her grandparents for coffee at the Ribarski restaurant. The childhood she described was wrapped in comfortable love. When the war was over, she had no one to play chess with and so she set up a board alone and analyzed games out of old books to pass long, sleepless nights.

I said, Let's play by telephone when I go back.

Seven hours apart. Late evening for me and the middle of the night for her. Edina liked to play on Saturday nights. She sometimes teased me about not having anything better to do, and I said, I have a child, I like to be home, and sometimes she asked me about Kosmos, why could I not get him to move to Toronto, and did I not miss him?

I always said the same thing: He loves *you*.

But he likes to sleep with you, she said.

Maybe he would be a terrible husband.

She laughed, Of course he would. But he is the father of your child.

Between us was a thing that could not be resolved. What was it exactly? Kosmos? Her war suffering? My warless life? We were drawn to each other, and we talked about our work and our daughters and mothers and mint gardens and writing and reading and chess.

During those six years of telephone calls, she consulted with the lawyers from The Hague about her files. We battled with our queens and knights and pawns and she told stories of her life, in fragments, each version never quite the same. We told each other the things we worried about and some of the things we loved. One late night she said, I am not afraid to die but I *am* afraid my life will disappear.

I thought, There is only the lifetime burning in every moment.

I said, Sometimes I think it is your own words that will immortalize you.

Who will hear them?

Someone, I said.

And then, because friendship is there for comfort too, I joked, Are you trying to make me too sleepy to beat you?

You have all eternity to sleep, she said. Let's play.

WHEN I MET her in Vienna with her mother, Esma, and her daughter, Merima, we liked to walk in the Lainzer Tiergarten, and each time made our way to the observation tower. Edina said she enjoyed this country-in-the-city and she imagined that in Canada there were many parks like this. I told her that in some we saw wildlife, elk and moose and bears in more remote places, and that even in my large city I had seen mink on the waterfront and raccoons were everywhere. Edina laughed and told me to stop teasing her and telling her such outrageous stories. She was relaxed in Vienna. Then, as if reading my mind, she said, My nightmares do not care what country I am in. I have them here too. I never escape them.

IN SARAJEVO, I slept at Edina's when I wasn't with Kosmos. He didn't have a home, only a room in someone's house, so he had fixed up the projection room at his small theatre for us with a mattress on the floor and some posters. Edina told me his family's apartment got taken over by others and he had nowhere to come back to. I liked making love with Kosmos under the flickering images of movies playing below.

I said to him, You have never told me about your family.

I had an older brother. I had my first cigarette with him. Let's go for a drive.

He liked to go up the mountain and look over the city. He

liked to walk along the old bobsled track and look into the woods and over the valley. We could not walk through the forest below because it had not yet been demined.

Kosmos said, My brother's body is still missing. He was fighting to the west. My parents died before him.

After great sadness, silence is not enough. But I did not know what to say.

I SOMETIMES TRAVELLED by bus with Edina to small towns outside Sarajevo for her fieldwork. She said she wanted dignity for women who had been pushed to the sides. At least, having told their stories to someone, to her, they would not die with a locked box inside them. She told me that before the war she used to watch the news coldly, and she thought little of it when she saw footage of refugees walking with nothing from one place to another. But now when she watched television images of war and migration she could feel their hunger and cold and fear.

At the bus station she warned me about a former soldier in this town who had acquired a white UN van for his personal use. He had mounted a skull on the hood and he drove around drunk threatening people through his open window. She pointed him out to me. The night of the second day, after dinner, as we walked through the dusk toward our little hotel, out of nowhere the white van drove by, honked at us, and the soldier shouted Edina's name. When he was past us, Edina said, I wonder if that is my father's skull.

I never got used to her ragged thought. There were things in her life that she could not make normal and when they erupted they tormented her. She preferred to tell jokes or to play chess. She said that when she used to tell Merima stories she always began, *Do you know the old fairy tales?*

Before the war.

Foča, Sarajevo

THE SARAJEVO CLOCK TOWER stands beside the tallest minaret in the city, where it has marked lunar time for five centuries since the age of Gazi Husrev-beg. The gilded clock hands set the moment of the coppery call to prayer. They have been reset every three days by the same man for the past sixty years. This man has attended to the ceaseless and uneven turning of earth and moon and sun, and only once during the siege did he fail to climb the tower's seventy-six steps to set the time for prayers. Time is no healer, and in the clock, storytelling and history have become one.

Edina began, Do you know the old fairy tales? There was once a golden time in our small villages in the mountains when people listened to stories of djinn and witches and evil lords and angels who sit on the left and right shoulders.

In those days, Edina said, my mother kept a small shop where she sold tinned and dry goods, soaps and stamps and pens, and listened to the gossip of our town. She grew up on a small farm with goats near the main road to the village, and my grandmother still lived there alone after her husband's passing. My father was a woodworker who built furniture during the days and whittled wooden birds in the evenings. I had no brothers or sisters and I played on a bend in the river with friends from the Lepa Brena apartment where we all lived. My mother's shop was nearby and across the road was the Women's Anti-Fascist

Club. We used to play ringe-ringe-raja, falling with great drama to the sidewalks from the imaginary smell of Uncle Paja's rotten egg in front of the old women. We could not imagine how these stiff creatures with swollen ankles and varicose veins had ever been revolutionaries. Over the river was a restaurant with a wide open-air balcony where our family gathered with our neighbours to celebrate birthdays and holidays, Kurban Bayram and Christmas Eve and Prvi Maj. On Sundays we walked to my grandmother's farm past tall sweet-smelling haystacks packed loosely, like soft mountains, to help my grandmother churn butter and stir and press her famous goat cheeses.

As I grew older I went on hikes with my friends to the woods of Buk Bijela and along the road to Trebinje throwing pebbles and counting the roofs by their shapes. Serb farmers preferred the flattened line to the full triangle on the roofs of their Moslem neighbours. It was a relaxed life, with lots of visiting and coffee. During festivals, the women put on aprons and embroidered blouses for the kolo dance. We all knew it, though we young people laughed at it. We played soccer and I sang in the choir and I acted in plays at the Partizan Sports Hall. Once we even took our play to the neighbouring village of Miljevina near the railway hotel. I knew girls from many households, the Karamans, the Bogdanovićes, the Lazićes. Our families had lived there for generations.

In high school I used to sneak into the second-floor classrooms with my friends by running across the cement bridge over the gully, then up the fifteen steps to the back door. I smoked my first cigarette in the forest behind, and many of the girls had their first kisses there too. Not me. Ivan took me for a long walk along the river and he held my hand and he said, This river is our destiny and the history of our blood.

I liked how he wanted to talk like a poet and a soldier, and I knew he was gathering his courage to kiss me. I had chosen him already and I wanted to go with him to study at the university. More than anything else I wanted to become a lawyer ever since I saw the American program about the lawyer in a wheelchair called *Ironside*. My mother who did not complete high school was happy I would do more. When it was time for me to leave for the city, my father gave me his own old copy of *The Damned Yard* because he had always loved those stories. He embraced me and said, Do not look where the harvest is plentiful but where people are kind.

My parents approved of Ivan Pašić. In the evenings when I studied, he sat with my father and tinkered with radios and clocks. Our two families invited each other to our homes, and at Christmas, Ivo made sure that I was served the secret coin in the česnica cake and on the first day of Muharram, I served him and his parents my mother's lamb ćevapi. I think that my parents hoped that Ivan would protect me in the city though they said nothing of this. Girls were freer than when they were young. I remember the night before we left on the bus, my father whittled a falcon from a piece of wood and he gave it to Ivan and said, I wish that my daughter might have someone to watch over her with vision as sharp as this wonderful mountain bird.

Ivo blushed.

The bus from Foča to town took about three hours, a journey of light and dark through tunnels carved into the mountains along the old Austro-Hungarian railway. There is a jutting orange rock that everyone from Foča looks for on the way to and from our small village. They call it *Stari čovjek*, Old Man. I used to look for him each time I returned from Sarajevo because when I saw him, I was almost home.

I loved my new life in the city and in law school and I thought of myself as one of the "new primitives." I listened to Patti Smith and Talking Heads and Sonic Youth and Idoli and I went to Kusturica's films with flying brides and gypsies. Ivan and I met Kosmos at an art show and became friends. He used to perform outside at the People's Theatre with his collective and he would walk down the steps into the crowd to deliver his lines to me. He was always crazy and hanging around me and I used to laugh at him and tell him if he wanted to be friends with me he had to be friends with Ivan too. We went to the same openings and poetry readings and on warm evenings made the long walk from the university to the terrace of the Bijela Tabija restaurant before the moon disappeared.

A student was arrested for walking naked down the street and calling his performance "Balls on Asphalt." Ivan helped make a performance of John Cage's 4'33" with twelve radios and lots of screeching and static. At the performance, Kosmos was drunk and called Ivan Radio-man, and I felt jealousy between them so I took both their hands and said, Let's dance.

When the dancing was over, Ivan wanted to be alone with me and we took the cable car up to the Vidikovac café to sit side by side on the patio overlooking the city.

It looks like a toy village, he used to say. And we are living miniature lives inside it. Are you happy?

Always at the end of each day, no matter where we had been, we found each other.

In law school I learned a new word, *privatnost*. It was an unfamiliar idea. At home we knew all our neighbours and we were each other's *kum* and I told Ivo everything. In the city we explored together, wandered through alleys and plucked young sloe berries from between the thorns, walked on the boulevard and ate crescent moon–shaped doughnuts.

One night Ivo said, Let's stop at the mosque.

He often had these whims and I was comfortable with him and with cupped hands we drank at the fountain as we had many times before.

Then Ivan said, I want to quench my thirst with you forever.

I did not laugh at him because I saw in his eyes that he was trying to say something important to him and I took his damp hands and asked, What is it, Ivan?

It is nothing.

But it is something.

I want to marry you.

Oh, this thing, I thought, that has been bothering him since we were children. First I felt it on the sidewalk outside Lepa Brena when we tossed stones, and then I felt it under the bridge by the Drina. I had already given myself to him. My friends used to laugh at me and say, You don't even want to look around? How will you know? But I knew and I said to him, I want to marry you too.

Always he was worried about something, studies, his parents, the sinister rumblings of politicians, things I paid no attention to.

WE TOOK THE bus to Foča, and with our parents and a few old neighbours, we had a ceremony at the town hall. I asked our neighbour's little daughter, Hana Begović, to hand a flower to each guest. After the certificates were signed, everyone had dinner in the restaurant near Lepa Brena, and while we danced, I told him, *Volim te*.

Then he said, We will be married again tomorrow with our friends in the city. We will be married every day of our life together.

Kosmos was waiting for us at the bus stop in the city with a borrowed green car covered with red paper roses. He opened the door and said to Ivan, Off to the hanging.

He drove us up to the abandoned bobsled track where our friends were waiting with music playing on cheap speakers and champagne and šljivovica and cans of spray paint. They'd been spraying poetry on the cement walls and handed us paint cans. Ivan sprayed a big heart and put our names inside. I wrote underneath, *Zauvijek*, to tell him that we would be together always.

One boy was already drunk and he shouted, He who heeds the first word of his wife must listen forever to the second, and his girlfriend punched his arm and he pretended to fall over and someone put a traditional folk dance on the cassette player and everyone scoffed at something so old-fashioned, but we all knew the simple peasant steps and danced along the length of the bobsled track. At sunset, Kosmos called to the men, Time for *akšamluk*!

I told them, No men's drink time on my wedding day, and my friends said, No drinks without wives or we'll leave you and have our own drinks.

Then the men complained, But you won't marry us!

Kosmos pulled Ivo and me away to his decorated car and he drove us to the elegant Osmice hotel along the mountain ridge where none of us had ever stayed. He stopped at the front doors and said, Tonight I leave for Paris. When I am finished my play I will come back and hold your babies. There's a room in there for you. Happy wedding night, a gift from your friends. Go, enjoy. There is only one first time. May you have it over and over.

And then he sang for us a popular song, "Volim Te Budalo Mala," and he took his strangled heart away.

IT WAS SOMETIMES painful for me to hear Edina tell such intimate stories about Kosmos. I knew so little about him. Nothing of his youth. Nothing of who he was before he was an expatriate in Paris. Never could I love him with the familiar tenderness that Edina must have felt for Ivan, who she had seen grow from a boy into a man. But I loved Kosmos. And he loved Edina.

Each of us loved the wrong person.

WAR CREEPS UP. Loudspeakers. Broadcasts. Hate your neighbour. On the radio, hate mixed in with local reports. Weather. Hate. Community news. Hate. Music. Hate. Some lives are worth less than others. People shrugged. Propaganda, they said. As if words no longer mattered, said Edina. At first no one believed what was happening.

She said that Ivan's friend Danilo went home to visit, got conscripted and could not come back. Young men began to hide in apartments. She said that rumours were moving through the city like grass snakes. The taste of gunpowder. Beatings. On the radio, exhortations of malice. These things can happen anywhere.

Hate-voices were mixing into the air like the cries of birds and church bells and calls to prayer. Militia set up barricades around the parliament buildings and sniper positions were organized and thousands of city people went into the streets to face down the occupiers.

She said, Ivan asked me to stay home with Merima, but I said, No, I am coming. Our daughter was fourteen and we had always raised her together. On a cool early-spring evening when we should have been going for a stroll up the mountain, our little family joined a large crowd to push back the soldiers. There was sniping from unseen places. We heard that trainloads of people with the possessions they could carry were leaving the city. Ivan wanted me to leave too. I was annoyed with him. I had a job too, a life there too. But Ivan said he had already bought bus tickets for us to go back to Foča in the morning, just for a few days, until we saw what would happen, please, keep our daughter safe. Go, find our parents, he said, and he would come as soon as he got our money from the bank. I remember the warmth of his hands. I could never resist him. And so, the next morning, I took a bus out of the city.

It was the last bus.

In hours, the roads were blockaded and we were trapped. Soon they were burning Trošanj and Mješaja.

Ivo telephoned and said to me, I am joining as a radio operator so I can find you. I will come to you. I am coming to you, Edina.

Then the lines to Foča were cut.

Our homes were gone. We had been tossed into the air like ashes. Men go to war for honour and come home to forget. But when homes disappear, where do soldiers go? Ivan's parents were killed by accident the day the soldiers blew up the Aladza mosque. Ivan heard about it during military surveillance. He had to record his radio transmissions in children's notebooks with colourful covers because there was no paper. On the front of Ivan's was a smiling elephant with three balloons. His commanders took his information and gave it to the generals to plan how to kill. They ordered soldiers to bomb people to the edge of madness, to report how many packages done away with.

The din in his ears destroyed him. Every day there were orders to wipe out a whole people. One of those people was me. We had loved each other since we were children and he could do nothing to stop any of it, nothing.

Sarajevo, Foča, Toronto

EDINA SAID TO me over the telephone, You play white.

Where are you?

Vienna.

I said, e4.

Nf6, she said. They have indictments.

A different opening for her. I asked, Is this the Alekhine Defence?

Yes, she said.

I listened to her blowing out smoke. I asked, Indictments for your trial?

Yes, she said. My mother and daughter are going.

To watch?

To testify. Your move.

d3, I said. To testify?

I heard her light another cigarette and slide a chess piece across the board. She said, d6. I could picture her in her mother's small, perfectly tidy apartment. She said, Yes. I too will testify. Your move.

Nf3, I said.

e5, she said.

I felt fresh defiance in her voice. I looked at the board and I was trying to grasp what she was saying. If she was going to be a witness, the indictments must be for men who'd held her captive. Her mother and daughter had also been held by him?

I said, I don't understand.

It is not a difficult move, she said.

I mean about you and your mother and daughter testifying, I said.

We have decided to go on the record, she said. To speak.

I was staring at my pawn.

First they shot my father, she said. When they locked us in the Partizan Sports Hall, I told Merima to hide in the bathroom. Soldiers came in and one yelled, Where is your daughter? I tried not to answer and he was drunk and beating me. I could not raise my head. Then he lifted me by the hair and said, I will kill you. And we will find her anyway.

I must have looked toward the bathroom. I was half-dead. He dropped me and they took her and brought her back the next day.

I heard Edina stand, move away, come back.

She said, They locked me up in some filthy hotel and by the time I was taken back, Merima was gone. Fourteen years old. I did not see her again until after the war. They moved me to Karaman's house and my mother was kept in town. Once a woman told her they had seen Merima in the Ribarski restaurant, but not that she was there being traded. My mother was evacuated to Tuzla and she did not know if we were alive. Ivo paid a soldier to buy me and get me out in the trunk of a car. I would have died. He could not find Merima. In Vienna I found a few rooms above a café run by a Bosnian couple. I had an operation, my insides were so destroyed, and I got work washing dishes. Then, one miraculous day, Merima appeared. We had not seen each other for almost two years. She was sixteen. She was so thin.

The chess board was a blur.

She said, Your move.

I said, Edina, I did not know.

How could you know.

I am so sorry.

She said, Your move.

I said, g3.

Bg4.

Impossible to play. She had often startled me in the past when she got her bishop out like that. Bg2. Do not turn away.

Nc6. Then she said, Merima picked up German quickly. She accepted counselling. The settlement workers said that she has adapted well. One said to me, Women refugees make a home wherever they are. Your move.

Castle, I said.

Good, she said. Be7.

h3, I said.

She took my knight, Bxf3.

And I took her bishop, Bxf3.

Now her attack. She said, Qd7.

I said, Bg4.

She took my bishop with her knight, Nxg4. She repeated her old joke, I take your wooden sliver.

It was obvious to take her knight. hxg4.

I asked, Does Merima want to go?

No, she said. h5.

I moved, gxh5.

She slid her queen out to Qh3.

I did not see what was coming and continued on the wrong part of the board, played Nc3.

Edina said, My mother also does not want to leave Vienna.

She took the pawn that was blocking the rook, Rxh5.

She said, We will only be two days in The Hague. My mother starts reliving it all. She cries. Talks about my father, how they destroyed our family's farm of seven generations. And I tell her the soldiers who tortured us still walk the streets freely. Your turn.

Nd5.

She said, Not good. Qh1. Checkmate. My mother says, Merciful god, I want death. She says that she is alone and she can't learn German and she wants to go home. But she can never go back. There is no place to go back to. Who thinks of old people after a war? Their time is finished.

I listened to her sweep her pieces into a little cloth bag.

This is what I think, said Edina. She is alive in death. She dies every day the moment she awakes. Yesterday she said to me, I saw some pigeons outside my window and I thought, even birds have more hope than I do. You made a couple of mistakes in that game.

Then she hung up.

THE NEXT EVENING, I phoned Edina and told her I was going to Foča.

Why?

To prepare to write about the trial.

Never will I go to Foča, she said. You write. The world forgets us.

Light crushed by darkness. Torment to remember. Torment to forget.

—

84

I WAS AFRAID to go to Foča alone. Kosmos said, I will introduce you to Mak. He drives tourists everywhere. He drives for the UN. He drives politicians. He drives everyone.

You come, I said.

I am writing my play, Kosmos said. I like Sarajevo. Go see Mak.

MAK WAS RANGY with powerful forearms. He had lost most of the hearing in his right ear during the war. He was sixty-three but moved like a man twenty years younger. During the war he was on the front line around the city. When he could get gas, he left the fighting and drove his beat-up beige Zastava through the darkness to fill water containers at a hidden artesian well. The water ran in a trickle and he waited and dozed like a young wolf alert even in sleep.

He said, Across the line, a lot of them were poor farmers. Part-time fighting. Sometimes we stopped to trade cigarettes and ammunition with them. Then we went back and shouted insults and fired.

Mak drove me first to the Širokača and Hambina Carina Cemetery in Bistrik to see his brother's name in stone. I did not ask to go but he took me there. I traced my fingers over the carved names and Mak said, He died the third day of the war. I went crazy, I ran in front of bullets. Then I said to myself, If I die who will bring water to my two sons?

Mak's war is the emptiness in his right ear and his brother's tombstone. He drives foreign war crimes units who tell him about his own battles with their detailed maps and lists of names. He has memorized the foreigners' war, burial grounds along the roads, in the mountains, outside every town, their body counts, their estimates made by comparing shifting earth and lists of missing. He has chiselled the history of their war inside his skull. His sorrow he keeps elsewhere. I asked him to take me to Foča, but after the cemetery he took me to the tunnel near the airport.

He said, It got gold medal for architecture. I would give it golden bullet.

Why?

Why not a few inches higher? They make it so low, like for dwarfs.

Mak liked to talk. He said, Better to have a good time together than sit like stones, why be quiet like boring? Men got a pack of cigarettes a day to dig the tunnel. The scaffolds were two metres high and when it rained the water was up to the waist. On the Butmir side we came out and this old farm woman gave us a cup of water. Angel with two teeth.

He laughed. He had told his stories so many times they were fables. He said, Someone falls in the tunnel or too tired to go on and no way to pass. Just wait. I was stuck in there many times.

He drove me to a bunker where he'd fought snipers on the hill above the city. It was a hot day and we hiked through the fragrant grasses where sheep grazed. We might have been going on a picnic. I did not even recognize this small grass-covered depression in the ground as a bunker. He asked why I wanted to go to Foča. He had never been.

I told him about Edina and about the trial and the rapes.

He looked away, down into the city. He said, People know about this but do not say. I drive everywhere and first time anyone wants to go there.

I thought, Everyone has secrets after war. Mak's do not include rape. I do not think he could drive me if they did.

THE WAY TO Foča is a winding road through narrow mountain passes. Mak lit cigarettes, sipped water, worked the gearshift. He pointed out massacre sites that looked like pretty mountain meadows. He showed me barns and sports fields and ditches where people had been slaughtered. I admired a vista and Mak pointed, Thirty-three there.

Do you have to spoil every view?

He shrugged. I can be quiet. You want?

I told him I wanted to know.

The river Drina curves and widens and narrows through the summer heat. Everywhere were gullies where men had killed each other and women had huddled under leaves, holding their breath, hoping not to be heard. When the boots stopped, there were shots and unzipping. After a hairpin curve, Mak pointed to a hill below the road. He said, Seven hundred buried there.

What does your name mean?

Mak? It means poppy.

The flower?

My mother named me for the poet Mak Dizdar.

Do you know his poetry?

Everyone knows it. I know only the love poetry.

Tell me a poem.

Mak lit another cigarette on the curve, said, You want too much, translating poetry while I am driving.

Ahead, hanging by two back feet over the road, a dead goat.

For the restaurant, Mak said. To show they have fresh meat. You eat goat?

The poem?

He shifted his cigarette to his left hand, reached for his water bottle, took a sip. A soldier's habit, dampen the lips and tongue, don't take too much, there may be need later. He was watching the sharp turns for trucks. He said, This is from "Calypso".

I cry
Because your love makes a slave of me
Because of love not strong enough to free me
You cry

He looked across at me and said, Why quiet? Not good? Not good for getting a girl?

He liked flirting. He liked the energy.

I said, Excellent for getting women. How do you say *I love you* in Bosnian?

Volim te. Want to know it in French?

I know it. *Je t'aime.*

In Chinese, *Wo ai ni*, Indonesian is *Aku cinta kamu.* What language you like?

Italian.

We looked across the enduring mountains and he said, This is a country of angels. And devils. Next village we stop for a break, then Foča.

His hands kept us from flying off the cliff on this switch-back road. Hands that had dragged dying soldiers into bunkers and carried water and food home to his family under shelling and lifted up the front right corner of his brother's coffin.

Fingers that had pulled triggers and the pins of grenades. Hands that had released a still-living man hidden between other men's dead bodies. He gave him some water and then the man died.

Better not to die thirsty, said Mak. Better not to die alone.

Hands that kill. Hands that make love. Sunlit rapids over smooth river stones.

IN FOČA WE drove to the high school and to Partizan Sports Hall and we saw the rubble of the old mosque and we stopped at the Ribarski restaurant where women had been sold and traded like fish. A man reeking of violence strode directly to Mak and reached out for a handshake and Mak squeezed the bones hard and pulled him close like a mastiff looking for the neck. The man said something in a low, harsh voice and walked away.

Mak said to me, I don't know him.

Did he tell you to get out of town?

Mak shrugged it off and said, Why say things to a stranger only standing, looking in at a few empty tables? No use. Now we go to find your Karaman's house.

WE DROVE TO the train station in Miljevina and up to the farmhouses looking down on the little town. We drove back and forth along a narrow road, trying to match the two-storey house in my photo. Mak pulled over, studied the photo, the line of the mountain ridge below the new tree growth, the iron gate on the steep driveway leading into the house. He said that we could match the pattern on the gate if it was still there, distinctive, three rectangles side by side like art deco. Back and forth we drove along the road. Maybe they tore the house down. Mak pointed to a jag in the mountain ridge and pointed to it on the photo. Suddenly he spotted the gate, partially hidden by hedges at the bottom of a steep drive. He turned on the empty farm road and parked the car facing back toward the main road. He got out, scanned the steep bank of woods above us.

Are we okay?

Of course. I make valet parking for you.

Why so careful?

I crossed the road and walked down the track to the gate. I touched the ironwork, the heavy lock, and I studied the house, small windows on the second floor, a door on the valley side, not much yard, a bit of wild mint, rock, no paths to the village, all access only from above.

Nowhere to escape. Even if a woman could crawl out a window or open a door there was nothing but a steep drop. What did it feel like, the first drive down this isolated road, sitting between soldiers you knew were going to rape you? What did it feel like trapped in that house, looking out windows?

I heard boots on gravel. Up on the road, a stranger was crossing toward Mak, and I hurried back up the drive.

When the man was in touching distance he spit at Mak's feet. Mak straightened to his full height, not stooped as when he talked with me. He shifted in front of me and the man spit again, at my feet, his eyes hard on mine and if I had been alone I would have been very, very afraid. I did not move, like an animal taking stock. In this moment I decided. To stay. To risk being wrong.

To risk being right. After an unnatural pause, the man moved on down the empty road, kicking stones.

Let's go, said Mak.

OVER TIME I learned the women's stories. I learned how the lawyers had reviewed with Merima her first statement, given eight years before. The young woman told me a little about her counselling and how she had put the war aside in order to survive. To learn German. To go to school. To become someone not destroyed. She did not want to remember who she had been before Vienna.

Yet to testify, she had to remember. She had to speak.

Merima told her counsellor who was old with stern wrinkles between gentle eyes that she did not know if she had the strength for a trial. But she wanted to please her mother.

The counsellor said, You do not have to go.

Merima said, I do not want to be a victim.

The counsellor said, The shame is his, not yours.

Merima wondered what people wear to court, how long she would be away from university.

The counsellor said, A person must be loyal to who they are, no matter what happens.

Merima chose her best jeans and a white T-shirt and jacket in the style of Austrian students. Her grandmother could not travel alone and so she would take her. She told her professors she had appointments. She was twenty-two years old, and she had to dig up the fourteen-year-old she had locked down in silence. A young Austrian man was interested in her and she had told him nothing about her past or about the trials. She wondered if she might ever feel anything for a man.

She had decided to go to please her mother. She had decided to go because to remain silent would be her own soul's suicide. How much more did she have to suffer?

EAST, LIGHT OF the world. Death, in a world turned over.

On my last trip with Mak we travelled east. He said, I want you to see Srebrenica.

Through the mountains again, past simple farms and barns, then the large battery factory warehouse made into a barracks. Mak led me through empty rooms at the back, past pornographic graffiti in Dutch and English, to barns, to massacre sites. The memorial at Potočari was a wide white-capped sea of grave markers, rows of green-covered coffins awaiting burial and marble walls of carved names.

People squatted, some with hands covering eyes, others with hands palms up to the sky, in ancient postures of grief. Craftsmen were still engraving name after name. People were still collecting and identifying, bone by bone, arranging memory.

Even Mak was quiet on the drive home. I dozed and awakened as the wild mountain road disappeared into the tunnel on the east side of Sarajevo. I opened my eyes in darkness and abruptly we emerged from the tunnel into the city, as if we had passed through a curtain into a fairy-tale kingdom. Out of a nightmare and into a dream.

—

I WAS WALKING with Edina through the narrow streets of the old market when a crowd of drunken young men approached us from behind. Before I knew where she went, Edina disappeared into a shadowed corner like a scrap of paper. The men passed and she stepped out and we said nothing. It was a sultry evening and many people were out. We strolled and turned into the courtyard of the Baščaršija mosque. We sipped cold water from the stone fountain and Edina reached into her purse and showed me a black-and-white photograph.

In the photo she is young and slim with clear skin and a broad smile. She is leaning against a young man. His arms are wrapped around her and her hands are crossed over his. She looks easily into the camera lens, a young woman loved.

Edina traced her finger over the photo as if the skin on the young man's face was still warm. She said, Look what I lost.

What happened to him?

She put the photo back in her bag and said, I only wanted you to see him. Do not ask. I love a ghost.

WHILE I WAITED for the beginning of the trial I worked a lot for Jacques Payac. I took on freelance work. I edited, wrote advertising copy and saved money. I worked early in the morning and was home every day for Biddy after school and all through the evenings. I spent as much time as I could with her. She was fifteen and she wanted to know I was there but did not much want to be with me. Mostly I listened to her moving above me in her room. One night I slipped into her bedroom to talk and she was sitting between two cheval mirrors and I asked her what she was doing and she said, I am trying to figure out infinity.

I said, During the trial I will come back and forth but I will be away longer than other times.

Mam told me.

She did?

Biddy shook her head as if I were the child. She said, Where you're going is the place my father comes from, isn't it?

No, the trials are in The Hague, but they are about the war in his country.

She looked down the line of mirrors at the endlessly repeating girl.

She said, I want to know him. Try to find him.

You will meet him very soon.

She felt something in my voice and she kept looking into the mirrors and said to her infinite reflection, You found him, didn't you?

She knew, of course. Children watch and know. Biddy was becoming as separate from me as I was from Mam. What else did I not know about her? I told her that I had found him and that in a small way he was involved in the trial, and that when it was over we would go to him together.

When?

As soon as the trial is over.

Why did he leave us?

He was never really with us. And later there was war.

The long line of girls in the mirror were all nodding at the same time.

I said, Biddy, tell me what you are doing in school. I've been away too much.

I'm okay, she said. I'm used to it.

She liked astrophysics. She told me that Mam said she could

learn to fly. She said she wanted to go to Chile, to the star observatory in the Atacama Desert. She said that when she was older she wanted to work there.

I did not tell her the only thing I knew about the Atacama Desert which was that below the great dry skies, the women of Calama walked day after day searching for the bones of the disappeared of Chile. After seventeen years of searching they had found the mass grave of their loved ones. I did not want to distract my daughter's eyes from looking up.

I realized that I had been listening to Biddy in the motherway of many streams at the same time. I had missed things. My second heart was outside me now. She had been waiting too long to meet Kosmos. My silence had made her another casualty of war.

JACQUES PAYAC'S STUMP was getting itchier with age. He said the amputation had never taken root in his mind, that he often felt he could still get up and run for a plane, across a battlefield, through a hotel lobby. He put his cigarette butt in a tin can and asked, What's happening with the trial?

I gave him a bottle of slivovitz and told him about the indictments, and that they only managed to bring in one man, Žarko Dragić. Jacques rubbed the part of his leg where the prosthesis joined.

No matter what I do, he said, there is inevitable withering of the limb. I add socks. The most dangerous part of writing is listening. Most people do not understand this. Hearing testimony means never ever being able to forget. Beatings. Breasts slammed by men in a drawer. Cigarette burns. You will hear detail after detail. Once you have heard you cannot unhear. The women will have to begin their forgetting all over again.

Maybe they don't want to forget anymore.

Maybe. Or others don't want them to.

I said, I need you to help me publish it.

Young man, I run a travel magazine.

I did not speak.

Finally he said, Don't you have any other friends?

No, I said.

The Hague

I ARRIVED IN The Hague and took the tram from the train station to my new apartment on the fifth floor of a building overlooking the sea on Gevers Deynootweg. There were seven tram stops from there to the courts—Kurhaus, Scheveningseweg, Badhuiskade, Keizerstraat, Duinstraat, Frankenslag, and finally Congresgebouw—seven doors to the underworld. My balcony jutted into the sea winds. I unpacked two suitcases, one of books and another of clothes.

The tribunal's grey administrative building at 1 Churchillplein, once home to Aegon Insurance, was reflected in a large, shallow pool in front of the building. In the pool were three stark, skybound sculptures. High fences and long, curving drives limited any uncontrolled movement around the outside of the building. Inside were heavy metal doors and locked basement storage rooms. Much wealth had once been created in this place from insurance promises to buffer us against the things we fear and cannot escape—accidents and sickness and death. The building was now renovated not for unwelcome events in the future but to serve justice for events in the past. There were courtrooms, witness rooms, cells, a large library, evidence vaults and offices, all tightly monitored behind ballistic glass and locked doors.

I entered through the metal detector and slid my bag over a low counter toward an officer. At each metal and bulletproof threshold were young, scrubbed armed security men who spoke several languages. Their name tags: Adriaan, Cees, Karim, Lieven. I felt something in Lieven, caught his eye, as I passed by. Inside was a raised reception desk and a great hall and a wide staircase under the vaulted ceilings of last century's grandeur. The building was a many-doored purple martin house where people from eighty countries worked together, lawyers and case managers and legal assistants and language assistants and witness assistants and librarians and forensics experts and security people flying in and out.

The core of Karla's team would be three women and one man. She had already worked and travelled with Sue and Lise to build the case. Back in The Hague she brought in a crime analyst. Nita Tamang would oversee the database that linked witness statements to other evidence. The only man on the team was Jonathon Bailey, nicknamed Joop, a small-town Canadian who happened to be travelling in Holland when the tribunal was being assembled. He applied for a job as a clerk but Karla discovered his photographic memory and saw his computer skills and she learned he had grown up with three sisters. She said to him, as if joking, You must have sometimes had a problem to find a free bathroom. Joop laughed and said, I made a bathroom spreadsheet but they all ignored it. So I just went outside.

Karla knew she'd found her case manager, bright, organized, flexible, forgiving and funny. In her habitual way of making strings of words, she called the women and Joop her Foča-Frauen-team.

They began with a database to integrate witness statements from church and refugee groups, the International Red Cross, Edina's group and others in the region. Karla and Lise travelled to meet women in exile in Vienna and Istanbul and Ankara and London and New York and Hamburg and Sydney and Toronto.

The women had precarious new lives. New languages. New jobs.

There was fragility.

I am afraid if I testify I will be killed.

I need my job. I cannot leave.

I am caring for my children, my old mother.

I do not want to remember.

Will *he* be in the courtroom?

Karla carried a soft, battered locked briefcase full of the women's words. She studied the files, mastered their detail. Memory is most accurate about place. *I was taken to Foča High School where I was a student the year before. A group of soldiers came into the classroom and picked eight of us. One took me to a small room and told me to strip.* Karla understood that she was disturbing a lightless world. *There were three hundred of us. I spent four months in that hall. It is a nightmare that cannot be understood.*

After reviewing three thousand files, Karla and her team finally settled on sixteen witnesses. Their stories were linked, all in Foča, the same perpetrators. The women were chosen for their place in the pattern of attacks and for their ability to withstand questioning. Karla wanted to show that the perpetrators' intent was to destroy a community by using women across generations. She wanted to begin her prosecution with Edina, her mother and her daughter. Three generations of the same family. The other thirteen women's stories would corroborate times and places and demonstrate the scope of the crimes.

The witnesses worried about live transmissions. Many did not want their families at home, in whatever countries they were living, to know. *I begged the soldiers to kill me but they laughed. They said, We don't need you dead. You will have our babies.* Memories of lost husbands stirred the women's anguish as much as living ones. Some men supported their wives and some refused to live with them after the war. Some women did not want their children to know. No one's peace was ever to be restored.

The voices of the witnesses would be altered on the transmission and their faces blocked with a pixelated mosaic. Only people inside the courtroom would see them.

Karla listened and absorbed the women's suffering and rage. But never could she fully know what their torment was. No one could. And she could not predict what might happen when a woman sat under the gaze of three black-robed judges, rows of lawyers and assistants for the prosecution on her right and, unseen but felt, the public gallery behind her. How would a woman tolerate the eyes of the accused on her, with his lawyer and security officers on her left?

Women were reluctant to leave the difficult new lives they had painted over their old lives. At the last moment would they even show up? Who could say what would happen in this new court?

Karla told them, I refuse to allow your testimony to fall into silence, shame.

The women did not know how to believe her.

Who, if I cried out, would hear me?

Lawyers talk about the rich narrative of a story in court, but anyone who has participated in a trial knows there is no rich narrative in the way that storytellers think of one. There are really only fragments of a mirror selected for legal battle. Its reflections may once have been the life, but no matter how carefully the fragments are put back together there are cracks. We labour to understand what has been lost between the silvery shards.

ONE SUNDAY MORNING in The Hague I visited the Celestial Vault, an outdoor art installation, a peaceful, grassy crater that people enter through a curving underground tunnel. At the centre of the crater is a sloped stone bed with two rounded stone pillows on the bottom edge. I was lying head down and looking up to see the crater's rim, to see the illusion of the sky as a vast sheltering dome. I wanted to bring Biddy here one day.

I was looking at the clouds when a woman approached quietly and said, Hello. Please, I do not want to startle you.

I sat up and recognized Karla.

I slid off the stone couch so she could try it. She lay down and said, Ah yes, I see. It feels like the sky is an umbrella.

We walked a little and chatted. She was curious about what I was doing and I told her I was writing about the trials and my friendship with Edina.

She said, I cannot talk to you.

We don't have to talk about the trial, I said.

I cannot talk about it with journalists, she said.

I understand, I said. Well, I'm taking the bus back to town.

And then, surprisingly, she said, I have my car. Come. I will give you a ride.

This is how I came to know her. She liked people and wanted to know them and was prudent but generous. Later she would tell me that as the trial had dragged on, and she saw me day after day in the public gallery, she had experienced my presence as hopeful when it sometimes seemed that the world no longer cared. Or worse, when it scorned the work.

But that day in the privacy of her car, I asked her why she had come to work in The Hague.

She remembered, she said, when her war was over, when she was twelve, coming back to a flattened Hamburg and seeing only the spire of St. Nicholas Church still standing. Her home was gone, her father's cobbler shop, her mother's bank, everything destroyed in Operation Gomorrah. At first, while they were setting up schools, her parents taught her at home. They told her about the concentration camps and the transports. They told her about the woman they had hidden in their attic who Karla thought was a distant cousin but was, in fact, a former customer of her father's. They had managed to keep her alive through the war.

In law school Karla fell passionately in love with Raphael, a survivor ten years her senior. For two years they were inseparable. He had been one of twelve people who showed up at the first meeting to rebuild the temple on Kielort Street. But he died suddenly, of a hemorrhagic stroke. Her beautiful Raphael, just gone. She was twenty-three years old and she was numb. After surviving so much, how could he die?

One must take things as they come, said her soft-spoken father, using the old German saying that she had heard since childhood: *Man muss die Dinge nehmen, wie sie kommen.*

When Karla met Andro, a quiet, ironic, rueful history professor from a region that had suffered war for centuries, she allowed him to love her. Andro was born in Croatia and educated in Hamburg. He loved music, the Beatles, opera. He had an academic's soft hands and mild slouch. He was lean with a small, rounded stomach. There was a deep furrow between his eyebrows not from worry but from concentration. He favoured two grey cardigans. He loved Karla, her ambition and confidence. The first time they had coffee together she told him she wanted no children. She wanted to pursue international banking law. Over their years together Andro's fascination for Karla did not wane. Her international work contrasted favourably with his own long days in libraries. She became expert in untangling secret accounts and tax evasion and businesses disguised inside hidden corporations all over the world. She joked, I am like an archaeologist brushing away layers of dust.

She said that on weekends she and Andro often went to the flea markets. He liked to collect small, lost domestic objects, old silver spoons, photographs, prints torn from books.

Karla stopped her car in front of my apartment building and I said, I hope the case goes well.

She said, It will. It will be like seeing the shape of the sky from a stone bed in a crater.

AT THE BEGINNING of the trial there were unexpected delays and hours to fill. I installed a long telephone cord in my apartment so I could pace. I read international law history and old court cases. The new court's *Rules of Procedure and Evidence* had taken nine months to write and I read them too. Everything was in the Peace Palace law library. I was much alone. I read about the presiding judge, Gladys Banda from Zambia, and about Judge Jack Smith from Australia and Judge Matteo Romano from Italy. In a world with few female judges I was especially fascinated by Judge Banda, who was the first woman in her family to be educated. She had switched to law school when she discovered there was no theology department at her university and found that she liked law. She was the only woman in her class. She taught, worked for the UN on the status of women, was a judge in Lusaka. I wondered who she was under the heavy gowns, under the rational reflection and tamped-down emotion. She had said in one interview that the reason she could have five children and her busy career was because of her husband. Gladys Banda believed every schoolchild should be actively taught how to make unpopular moral decisions, and to work through the logic behind them and to practise defending them. She said that her father, a villager with a grade-school education, always told her and her sisters and brothers, You have to look after wealth, but knowledge looks after you. I wondered how many rape trials Judge Banda had presided over in a place where traditional healers told men that sex with young girls, even relatives, would bring them health and success. Her favourite novel was *Woman at Point Zero*. I thought about the energy of this woman who had let nothing stand in her way, who had ruled on *kikondo* and witchcraft. She was ambitious. She would have to control a difficult and emotional courtroom. In another interview she had said, I am a good judge because I have been subjected to undue scrutiny. I am not talking about race but about being a woman.

Then the interviewer asked whether being a woman affected her views of areas of the law concerning women.

Judge Banda answered, Does being a man change his views on areas of law pertaining to men? The law is for everyone. A judge brings all their experiences to their work. If they have experienced discrimination—as a woman—they will be sensitive to its subtle expressions. A judge is the human conduit of the law.

WHEN I TIRED of reading, I visited galleries, walked along the beach on the cold Atlantic, saw the abandoned bunkers in Scheveningen. Thirty-three hundred troops had lived in them during the last war, alien underground conquerors who controlled the city from below. Large signs forbidding entry, *Verboden toegang*, were loosely nailed on the bunkers' doors and I easily stepped into the dank, abandoned place. Stretched ahead of me was a long, empty hall with stone walls, graffiti, the smell of dried urine and excrement and stale blood. I moved deeper into the tunnels, exploring rooms that were once offices and sleeping quarters for the young German men who had brought the country to its knees in a few days and forced the Dutch to build these bunkers with stone and shovels. The Dutch had to think of their conquerors eating and sleeping below them, as if they were enslaved by a city of ants. I entered a large room with a long, broken table and a cupboard that had once been a kitchen storage area. I looked for a cistern or some other way to collect water and then I saw a door, ajar, that opened into a high-ceilinged room. I pushed it open and saw hundreds of bats hanging from the ceiling, the floor deep in stinking guano, and I pulled back, startled. Was there a crack in the caves through which they escaped into the night air each dusk? Did they fly with their little human faces and hands outstretched through the tunnels I had just walked through? I examined the numbers and dates and caricatures young soldiers had scratched into the walls. And then I became aware of an odour and a movement behind me. A very old woman with tangled hair and dark eyes was staring at me. She wore a torn, filthy brown skirt and a purple sweatshirt. Her decayed teeth were brown under cracked lips but her eyes were oddly gentle. I said, Hello, *excuseer mij*, I do not speak Dutch.

I stepped back to show I meant no harm and then I said, Can you show me the way out?

She turned her back to me and began to walk away. I followed her through tunnels I did not recall and finally I smelled fresh air. In a few more moments I saw a slash of sunlight cutting across a corner and I realized she had led me to a different point of entry.

Why are you here? I asked.

She said, My daughter die. Here.

I am sorry. *Can I see another's woe, And not be in sorrow too?*

Long time, she said.

When?

In war, she said.

I am sorry, I said again.

Soldiers, she said.

I walked into the salt air. There are memories people cannot recover from. I longed for Biddy, for Mam. I thought, I will find a way to go home during the breaks. Take on extra work. I will find a way to be in two places at the same time.

AN ABRUPT SHIFT took place in the prosecution only two weeks before the trial was to begin. The senior trial attorney for the prosecution would be not Karla but a Canadian named William Steyn. Karla later told me how this happened.

She said, When I learned that the court administration had assigned a Canadian criminal lawyer to take the lead on my case, I was very angry at the whispers that my expertise in international white-collar crime did not transfer in court to violent war crimes. Or that I knew only civil law. None of the excuses made sense. I was furious. I had built the case, read thousands of files and travelled to three continents. I had won the confidence of our witnesses. Now a man was to take over all my work? I was so angry that I would have left The Hague if it had not been for the trust the women had put in me.

Steyn had never lived in Europe and spoke no language but English. He was so new he got lost walking to meet the team to review the case. He was the least informed in the room. But he had been assigned to lead.

Karla said, I knew that he was impressed as he watched Joop pull up files and papers before I asked for them, as he saw Sue show each woman's spreadsheets anticipating my next point. I had built a team that respected and liked each other and he must have felt my anger. But he only said, Thank you. Once I have read through the witness files, I will review with you my line of questioning.

I answered, This is not possible.

Karla had worked with many men like William Steyn, men accustomed to having authority. He said, It will have to be possible.

The witnesses expected to be questioned by her. They might not come at all if an unknown man would be questioning them. It had taken years to build their trust.

And then William Steyn did something she did not expect. He stood up and said he had a plane to catch. Karla asked where he was going and he said he was going to Foča and he would meet her again in two days' time.

He was met at the Sarajevo airport by three vanloads of military police to accompany his armoured vehicle. After a winding drive through the mountains on the old Austro-Hungarian routes, he was protected by 250 men from the French army who appeared at every side road in more armoured vehicles. They drove him past the destroyed mosque, past the high school, and they went with him into the empty Partizan Sports Hall up on the hill across from the police station. They visited the Ribarski fish restaurant and inside he was flanked by armed soldiers. Old men smoked and drank coffee and stared at him with centuries-old suspicion. He got back in the car and felt embarrassed by the level of security around him.

When he had asked if the security was necessary, that it felt wrong, his military escort said, Yes, sir, it is. Whatever you're feeling is probably right.

Hatred? he had asked.

Yes, sir, that might be right. We are not welcome. By the way, sir, here they do not call the town Foča. They call it Srbinje.

They drove him past two motels in town where women were imprisoned and then to Karaman's house where Steyn was escorted down the steep driveway, through the iron gate and into the empty two-storey mountain house. The house was dirty, with old blankets in corners, dry garbage in the kitchen. Back on the road, he nodded up the hill and asked what the soldiers were looking for.

Snipers, sir. We have to leave, sir, if you want to catch your plane.

Arrests had been difficult. One accused had tried to drive his car straight into the Stabilisation Force soldiers and they shot him. The second blew himself up with a hand grenade before he could be arrested. William had worked with a lot of murderers but this was a different landscape. He asked his escort, What was your worst fear taking care of me today?

The soldier said, You'd be shot.

William asked what would happen to a woman from there if she testified and then went back.

They'd probably kill her.

Karla said, Steyn asked me to have coffee with him in his office when he got back but there were no machines and he had no cups and he had to apologize that there was nothing to drink. He pulled a chair out from behind his empty desk to face the only other chair in the undecorated room and he said, I have been tasked with leading this case.

Karla smiled ruefully and said, How often had I seen men scoop up work done by others as their own. I knew how they feign temporary disadvantage if it meant a long-term win. But I did respect that he had gone to the crime scene. I saw that he was a formidable negotiator. He asked me, What do you want?

I intended to stick to my position. I refused any silly tit-for-tat games with him. I told him I did not want a man to lead. This was no game of tactics. Even the male investigators were a disturbance to the witnesses.

I told him, I want to interview all the witnesses.

I watched him control himself and then he asked, Which of the witnesses do you think would refuse to come if they thought they would be questioned by a man?

All of them.

That was when he told me about his visit to Foča. He understood that a lot of people would prefer us dead.

He said, Karla, I want to win this case. You take the prominent role in the trial.

I insisted to him that I would not give him any of the rape victims to question. People would not respond to his American directness. Naturally, he was a little insulted by this. I knew of course he was not American but I also knew that he had learned the history of the region from a BBC documentary. Then I discovered that he was pragmatic, and fair.

He stood and said, All right. You take the rape victims. I'll take the expert witnesses. Maybe give me one or two of the older women, so we do not show any weakness to the defence. We are going to win this together. Yes?

There was no turning back and the women were counting on us.

His first job was to write the opening statement and he asked me for advice, not to flatter me but because time was short. He wanted to know, as he put it, how to capture the human element.

Karla said to me, Always women must protect what is already theirs in bureaucracies. I have had to do this all my life. It is infuriating. I had been thinking about the opening statement for years. But I had to give it away for the larger good of the work. I told him I had planned to quote a woman who had said to me, *I had no control. I was like a machine in their hands.*

MERIMA WAS WITHDRAWN. Esma was tired. Fidgety. We sat in the Beach Club café at their hotel with Edina, drinking coffee and trying to relax. Their witness assistants sat nearby. The women had returned from visiting the courtroom and from

witness-proofing, the painful, meticulous review of their statements with their lawyers. Merima had asked her witness assistant to look after her grandmother. She needed to concentrate.
She needed quiet. I watched Merima half-turned away from our
table, staring over the ocean, her intelligent grey-blue eyes
drawn into the distant depths. She had her mother's eyes. But
more vulnerable.

Esma said to me, I brought wild orchid root and sugar and
cinnamon for us to drink with warm milk at night. It is good to
calm the nerves.

The old woman's large work-worn hands were restless and
her fingers unconsciously searched for a missing wedding ring
around her third finger. She said that she had never stayed in such
a luxurious place where she could look out her window at the
sea. Her witness assistant, Beatrijs, had offered to take her to visit
the miniature village or perhaps to walk along the beach to see
the big sculpture of the Fisherman's Wife, but the old woman
wanted to stay with her family.

Merima turned back to our table and said to me, My identification in court will be Protected Witness 81. That is the number
from my first statement eight years ago. But the name of the trial
is for *him*. We women remain nameless and his name is written.
Do you not find this ironic? I do.

She laughed without mirth. Her laughter was a wall to keep
people out. She touched her grandmother's arm and asked,
Baka, are you frightened of speaking in the court?

I am frightened of what I have to say.

Do not worry, you are strong.

Edina smoked. She nodded toward the assistants' table and
said to me, You are making people nervous.

I thought so, I said. I'll go now. I won't see you until after you testify.

Edina said, I will telephone. And I will know you are there behind the glass.

I finished my coffee in a single swallow, kissed each of them and left.

THE NIGHT BEFORE the trial began, I visited the public gallery. I looked into the empty courtroom through the glass, a body without a soul. The back of the witness chair was to us and much of the testimony would be made with the blind down over the window. I taped a handmade *Reserved* sign to a chair in the front row on the left. This was not permitted and it was gone in the morning when I arrived. When the blind was down, I would watch the trial on the monitors with pixelated images and altered sound. I needed to hear the caught breath and the emotion that trial transcripts do not capture. I wanted this corner of the gallery to be my safe perch. I had dreamed the night before of a living bird turned into a ceramic bird that slipped from my hand, cracked into pieces and turned into a handful of sapphires. The long dream was filled with mountains and eight-pointed stars and water and disappearances and crescent moons.

There was a movement at the side door of the courtroom. I saw, with surprise, Karla coming in alone. She walked to the desk that would be hers. She stared at the witness chair. Her short hair was uncombed and when she saw me she left the courtroom. A few moments later she came through the gallery door.

I asked, Are you nervous?

Why would I be? I have evidence.

I said, But much of the evidence will be the victims' words against the accused. And there is no case law about sexual confinement in war.

Karla walked the length of the window. She was looking at the courtroom from the world's vantage.

She said, After World War Two, there was a trial about rape.

I did not know, I said.

With sorrow and with hope, a plea of humanity to law, we cannot shut our eyes.

No one does. It has been kept secret. The trial was not held in Germany.

Why has it been kept secret?

To protect witnesses. Secrecy would have been their condition to testify.

But what use is it if the country, the perpetrators and the outcomes are all secret?

She said, This is how deep the shame goes.

I said, But secrets and silence encourage the tormentor.

The conscience of humanity is the foundation of all law.

I must go, she said. At the door she turned to me, Tomorrow the case will be on the record. For all of us.

Dragić (IT-93-01) ICTY

Protected Witnesses

(PW-21)	Meliha Subašić
(PW-24)	Hana Izetbegović
(PW-31)	Fuada Puškar
(PW-43)	Zehra Zlata
(PW-49)	Uma Hadžiosmanović
(PW-52)	Jasmina Begović
(PW-70)	Esma Sefo
(PW-71)	Edina Pašić
(PW-75)	Šefika Tvrtković
(PW-81)	Merima Pašić
(PW-91)	Nura Muslimović
(PW-97)	Hanifa Kalajdžić
(PW-186)	Nejra Kulenović
(PW-187)	Mubera Sokolović
(PW-199)	Rakifa Hafizović
(PW-212)	Šaha Imorović

JUDGE GLADYS BANDA leaned toward the microphone and spoke the first words of the trial: May the registrar call the case.

Mr. Hans Bakker rose from the registry desk. He wore practical leather dress shoes and a grey suit. He called the case number and he announced the reason they were there: The Prosecutor versus Žarko Dragić.

—

THE TURBULENCE STARTED the first morning of the trial. Čedo Milinković, the defence lawyer, turned his body slightly away from his client, Žarko Dragić. The accused was tall and dressed in a cheap, ill-fitting suit. His skin was weathered and greyish from continual smoking, with skin bagged under his eyes, a carved vertical scar on his right cheek and a deep wrinkle between his eyebrows. He moved with censored physicality. He was extremely self-conscious and had chosen to affect an expression of false submission. I had often watched our dog at home make this look. Dominated by someone in our small pack, Mam or me, she would lower her head and her ears and turn her eyes away, all the while watching us from the sides. Edina had told me that before the war Dragić was a village man known more for hunting and bumming cigarettes in the cafés than anything else.

The counts were read as part of the routine opening of any trial and Dragić had been instructed to plead guilty. But with unnaturally open eyes he stood and pled not guilty to the count of crimes against humanity.

I watched Karla look to the judges in surprise. Had they been aware? She had not been informed ahead. She should have been. The judges' faces remained impassive, though I saw heightened alertness in their eyes, always a slight dilation of the pupils that cannot be masked, and a tightening of displeasure in Judge Smith's jaw. He was already turning the pages of the indictments in front of him. Judge Banda asked Dragić to explain himself.

Dragić said, I hope you understand why I pleaded guilty. I have been listening to you read the charges. Will someone tell me where in these counts you are . . . in the paragraph nine, is that what you are all talking about? . . . and then I might be able to plead guilty, of course, taking into account the circumstances, the circumstances being war. I am trying to explain the amount of hesitation in my mind, and why I said I was guilty of one but not another. I tried to explain to my lawyer but I think he does not understand me or maybe believe me. Am I failing to make myself clear in legal terms, which I do not understand? I was misled, not knowing the law. I do not want to tell a lie at all. I came here to be honest, to be decent, to tell you what exactly I did, and it is up to you to say how guilty I am, and to mete out a sentence. I hope I have made myself clear.

His lawyer looked at the judges as if to say, You see what I am dealing with. He thinks he can endear himself, plead directly with you. Then the lawyer lifted his palms to the ceiling as if to say, Why does he not know that this is not the way of the court?

Judge Smith turned another page, thinking, and in a firm voice told Dragić that of course he had the right to speak in court but that he strongly advised the defendant to use his counsel. He asked Dragić if he understood what he was pleading guilty to. He slowly explained, unfolding one finger at a time from a closed hand as he spoke: the components of a crime against humanity are three—an attack on human dignity, attacks on civilians, and part of widespread or systematic attacks.

Dragić must have believed, in the first hour of his trial, that he was in control of his destiny, that a trial was a conversation between him and a judge. His eyes were so wide open that the whites were visible all around their frantic dark centre.

He said, I am only trying to tell the truth. I did not understand the words *systematic attacks*. I raped but I did not do that.

This man who laboured over writing his name, who could hardly read, was revealing too rich a narrative for the court, one that was beyond its conventions. He was making the court after his own image. Dishevelled. Disorderly. Too human in its confusion. No one had foreseen a confession in the first ten minutes of the trial, even the lawyers with their training in twists and quiddities. It would not be seen as justice. It was intolerable and had to be contained.

Judge Banda ordered a closed session with the lawyers, and court was adjourned.

THE NEXT DAY, I watched everyone arrive back in court. Karla was beside Sue and William, and the interpreters settled themselves in their booth above, where they worked in pairs and alternated every half hour. From their glassed-in room at the same level as the judges' desk, they could see the whole courtroom. In the rows of desks below were the clerks and legal assistants. Nita and Joop sat near the witness chair. Dragić entered between two security officers, but his lawyer's chair was empty. All rose for the three judges.

Judge Banda asked everyone to sit.

Then the court was informed that the defence lawyer had disappeared from The Hague.

Dragić stood and said, I want to represent myself. I will tell the truth and that will be to the prosecution's advantage so they can quickly finish this case. Only I know what really happened, but I need to ask some legal questions. I have no one to get legal ideas from.

Karla looked at the judges with swift intention, poised to object, eyebrows raised. Who would take control? Judge Smith assured Dragić that this was his right. He assigned him a temporary counsel and Judge Banda adjourned for ten minutes for them to meet.

When they returned Dragić said he wanted a counsel. Judge Banda made rebukes, demanded apologies for the record and then turned to Dragić and told him briskly that a new counsel would be found for him.

Court was adjourned for three weeks.

I WALKED THE long way home, breathing in salt air. I phoned Jacques Payac from my balcony overlooking the sea. I said, The trial is delayed. I'm going to Sarajevo to see Edina for a few days, then I'm coming home. Can you give me a few weeks' work?

Jet-setter, said Jacques. Young man, what is this trial about?

About the women.

More detail.

About violence.

What else?

I am not going to call you anymore if you do this.

Yes, you will. What else? What are you going to write about a defendant who says he was only following orders, or about a defence lawyer who can't control his own client? They will say the generals knew nothing. Tyrannical regimes are captive to their own lies. But the law too can be a tyrant.

I will resist those lies, I said. I will dispute the tyrannical habit of pretending not to pretend.

How?

By telling the truth. I want Edina's story engraved in the air we breathe.

All right, young man. Come home. I need a lively feature on

how to pack for carry-on. *Fais de beaux rêves.* By the way, I got you a free air pass for a year. *Ciao.* See you soon.

I FOUND EDINA and Kosmos in the lobby at the Sartr Theatre on Gabelina Street. Kosmos said, Come, see where we watch the trial.

On the stage were two old chintz-covered armchairs once used as props. In front of them was a small television on a chest of drawers. Kosmos had told all the actors that he and Edina would use the stage during the days until the trial was over.

The actors argued, What about our play?

He laughed at them and said, Eat shit. You can have the theatre at night.

Eat it yourself, they said to him, but they left.

We sat on the stage and had coffee together and Kosmos said, I do not want to watch alone in an office. Here at least are hairy-balls actors complaining in the halls.

Edina said, I like my office.

I will stay with you, said Kosmos. After the trials I will write my play. Right now I am too fucking sad.

Edina handed me a cake.

I felt how close they were. I also felt the strangeness of their war being retold in a faraway court. In a foreign language. Under a foreign system.

I told Edina this and she nodded but Kosmos said, I like that shit-on-your-sunshine court.

We both had to laugh.

She said, They'd never do it here.

—

EVERYWHERE IN SARAJEVO, people were half watching the trials, adjusting screens and volume, complaining, gossiping, lawyers take more breaks than our politicians, why no America?

People went for walks, to the park to watch men playing chess on the big chessboard with pieces each a metre tall. They called out jokes and mocked each other. One player took three pieces in a row and said, Now I have enough wood to keep me warm all winter.

At the end of the game his opponent cursed him across the crowd, It was the first and last time in your life you will win.

People walked along the river. Workers were rebuilding the National Library and the Oriental Institute after four months of devastating bombs. They were once again raising the dome and painting two thousand square metres of arabesques on the walls. But the beautiful books were gone, the rare manuscripts and incunabula, all ash, all gone.

KOSMOS BROUGHT US burek pastries and coffee in small porcelain cups. Edina set up her chessboard on a low table between the two chairs on the stage and turned the black side to me.

I sleep badly, she said. I wanted the trial to be over. Now I must go back. What will you do?

I am going home till it starts again.

She lit a cigarette with stained fingers. She said, I should go to Vienna. But I want to be alone. I stay in my apartment. Kosmos comes to me but we never meet like light-squared and dark-squared bishops. My family is destroyed. When one family is damaged, all are.

What could I do? Listen to her. Play chess. I had foreign

money. I was sleeping in her apartment. I put enough money on the table for her to travel to Vienna.

She looked at me and I said, Just in case you want to go.

She played her opening move, e4, and I played e5.

We continued to play quickly until I got into trouble: Nf3 f6; Nxe5 fxe5; Qh5+ Ke7; Qxe5 Kf7; Bc4+ d5; Bxd5+ Kg6; h4 h5; Bxb7 Bxb7; Qf5+ Kh6; d4+.

She looked at the board and looked at me to see if I had seen the check from the bishop. I had. I resigned.

I have replayed that game in my mind. The ways it could have gone. I have often thought of the thousand moves we can make and how easy it is to make the wrong one.

We put the pieces away and I said, Sometimes at home I go to get my fortune read.

Why?

I don't know. To change how I feel. To hope.

She considered this and said, I don't hope.

I know.

She reached across the table, took my coffee cup, turned it over, then righted it to examine the patterns of the grounds on the white porcelain.

She tipped the cup so I could see the streaks and she said, Tears.

She tamped her thumb on the bottom of the cup. She showed me an imprint like a mandala. She licked her thumb and said, An evil eye.

I said, You don't know how to read coffee grounds.

She set down the cup and laughed a true and open-throated laugh. She said, You're *drska*.

What does that mean?

Like, bold.

She had left a burning cigarette on the ashtray while she pretended to read my cup and forgotten it, and now she took another from the package and lit it.

I said, So you smoke two cigarettes at a time now.

She shrugged.

MR. MOCHAN MATARUGA was Dragić's new tribunal-assigned attorney. Those who could not afford counsel in these international trials were provided with lawyers who, like anywhere, ranged in integrity and ability. Mataruga wore an expensive suit, had practised in Germany, stood legs apart like a boxer. I saw a man who loved his own authority. He had no fear of controlling his client. This time when Dragić rose he pled not guilty.

Denied the rapes. Denied everything.

Now the trial was under way.

DAY AFTER DAY behind the glass, the personalities of the people in the courtroom revealed themselves. Joop kept lozenges and tissues and some extra pens and a photograph of his girlfriend in a little wooden cigar box. Karla habitually looked up at the interpreters as if urging them to do better. Mataruga was a pen tapper.

It takes hours to establish fact and detail and context in a trial. The interpretation was simultaneous but there were pauses as people worked between English and Bosnian, Croatian and Serbian, which the court referred to as BCS. Witnesses could be unsettled by accents. All through the region people judged others by how they spoke and their names. I gave nicknames to the judges. Judge Banda was Demeter because her neutral eyes were peering into hell. Judge Smith was Starman because the Elmo projector annoyed him and one day he said with impatience that light from distant Sirius A would illuminate the images better. Silent, precise Judge Romano was Federico, for the famous Italian director who said that the barrier between the conscious and unconscious is not very great. To pass the time, I taught myself to sketch from a little book called *How to Draw Faces* that I'd found in the antiques market.

Judges train their bodies toward stillness under heavy black robes but the eyes continue to communicate intention, concern, confusion, determination. I watched the judges' impassive faces for any movement at all. Only Smith, the least patient of the three, did not seem aware of a slight deepening in a light frown line between his eyebrows.

My brother called to ask, How is the trial?

Like watching paint dry, I said.

Trials are slow, he said. I'd like to see an international court someday. Write down some good quotes for me. Is your guy there?

Who?

Biddy's dad.

No, I said. Listen, go see her for me.

I do, said my brother. Every Sunday.

KARLA CALLED THE first witness, Esma, PW-70. The blind was down in the gallery. I imagined Edina's mother entering the strange room and sitting at the witness table in the middle of the courtroom. I imagined her placing her feet in her polished leather shoes squarely on the floor. And I imagined her glancing over to see *him*. Above her. On her left.

I wondered if he remembered her at all.

The old woman swore to tell the truth and confirmed her number, and Karla asked her to describe where she was when the war began.

Esma said, We hid in the woods. The soldiers found us in a hollow and they shot my husband and they cut off his ears and they threw him in the Drina and they took me and my daughter and granddaughter and some neighbours too. They took all of us to the workers' huts at the gorge, Buk Bijela, and they lined us up against the walls and a soldier came and got me and he showed me my husband's bloody clothes and he took my wedding ring, and then he offered me a cigarette and said, Grandmother, you come with us. I heard women screaming and I knew what was happening in the other huts and then it happened to me, he said to teach me, and we were all crying and they took us in a bus into town to the high school. The next day they moved us to the Partizan Sports Hall.

Karla showed Esma a piece of paper with witnesses' names and numbers. She asked her to identify, using their numbers, which women had been with her.

Esma took the paper. To decipher the letters, she pronounced the names to hear them aloud. In the gallery I heard her familiar voice whispering, and then suddenly Mr. Mataruga was saying loudly and with great agitation, Please, Your Honour, the microphone is on. The women's names are being broadcast.

Judge Banda called a recess, said they had not anticipated this. They would create a time delay for the broadcast. Esma was escorted out of the courtroom, ashamed of her mistake. She was sure she had ruined the trial.

Beatrijs was waiting for her and she said, Esma, do not worry. You are helping us to see how to do this. You are first. We must all learn to do things correctly.

Esma said, I will not do it again. I can read quietly too. My husband has no grave but the Drina river.

Beatrijs said, Esma, you are irreplaceable. You are why we are here.

Edina told me that her mother awoke strangely refreshed the next morning.

In court Esma was able to read with no sound, only moving her lips a little, and she listed the numbers of all the women she knew, her daughter, PW-71, her granddaughter, PW-81, her neighbour, PW-91, and thirteen others from her village.

Karla asked her to repeat what the accused had done to her.

She said, He had his way.

Karla said, I know it is difficult to say. In the court it is all right to use the formal words.

Esma said, He showed me the bloody ear of my husband. He took my wedding ring. He raped me.

Thank you, said Karla.

Esma said, They did it to fill us with terror.

Judge Banda said, Please, Witness. Only answer the questions as they are asked to you.

I imagined that Karla would be looking at her with warm eyes, trying to keep her confident. She proceeded through a series of simple questions.

At Partizan Sports Hall were there toilet facilities?

Yes.

How would you sleep?

Well, on the floor.

With blankets?

No.

Were you fed?

Once in three days. We gave the food to the children. The camp was filthy.

Thank you, Witness.

NOW MATARUGA HAD to cross question and dismantle the woman, prove her unreliable. He had humiliated her already. Illiterate. Easy to crack her like a dry stick.

He said, You are using the following expressions, camp and prisoners. When somebody tells me that he is a prisoner in a camp, I think of something quite different. But you said in your statement that you were taken to the Partizan Sports Hall. How is this a camp? It is a community centre.

We were prisoners there.

But it is certainly not a camp.

We were imprisoned there.

And yet it was a recreation hall with several doors and windows that opened.

Judge Smith interrupted, Counsel, the witness is telling us what the place was like and how they were treated. Now, you don't argue with her.

Mataruga pressed his lips together and checked the clock. Here, in this foreign court, his usual strategies of intimidation and mocking were curtailed. Implied threats were not permitted. No money or handshakes behind doors. Rule 96 stated no corroboration was necessary for the testimony of victims of sexual assault. It was a difficult case.

To gain a little time he said, There is distortion in my headphones. Instead of hearing the voice of the witness, I hear the interpreter.

The registrar said, You must use the button on your desk to control the channels and the volume.

Mataruga was obsequious, said, Your Honour, please forgive me.

He turned back to Esma. Let us clarify matters, he said. When you gave your first statement, were you telling the truth? Did you say you were in a camp?

I always tell the truth.

Yes, I do believe that you did tell the truth at that time. What did you say?

I told them what happened, how they dragged us away and put us in the camp.

Do you know that everything that we're saying here today is being recorded?

I know that.

Well, you're unwell, let's make a break.

No.

I'm suggesting only for your well-being.

No. What I know, I will say. What I don't know, I cannot say. You cannot make me say anything I don't know. I've had enough of all this.

I do believe that you have had enough. You lived through a war.

What I know, I know. What I don't know, I don't know. A camp is a camp.

Mataruga gestured to Dragić, You see this man here? He has been charged with terrible crimes.

Esma said, He committed terrible crimes. They killed my husband. Now I must live in a foreign country. They took the wedding ring from my finger.

Mataruga looked up at the judges. Waited.

Judge Banda said, Please, Witness. Only answer the questions.

I LEARNED TO see tiny changes in Judge Banda's neutral face. When the lawyers were hard on witnesses her lower lids tightened and she swallowed and the corners of her lips compressed. Justice must be *seen* to be done. It was too early to feel annoyed by the defence's tactics, and yet she did. This witness had brought sincerity and outrage into *her* court. This witness had suffered enough. But there must be process.

I thought, She listens as a judge and a woman. Her eye sees what others might miss.

She said, Counsel, ask her questions only to elicit the evidence. Otherwise we will be here forever.

His skin was dry and hard, and he answered, Perhaps I've let myself go a little, but Your Honour, I ask your indulgence. We come from those regions, we are part of the same fabric. I know everything this woman has gone through.

This Esma would not stomach in silence. Žarko Dragić, who sat looking down on her, had done terrible things to her granddaughter and daughter. She would not listen to his filthy lawyer with his smooth tongue.

She interrupted, *Od istog materijala!* We are not the same fabric. He knows nothing of what I went through. I lost everything. He understands nothing about me.

Judge Banda had to control her courtroom. Already this was

proving difficult with traumatized witnesses. I wondered if I detected in Mataruga a masked disdain for her, a foreigner, a woman, an African. I wondered how often she had encountered prejudice throughout her impressive career. Whatever she felt, she showed no emotion. She would not allow herself to be seen as less than impartial.

She said, Witness, we understand. Would you like a break?

No, and I don't want to be provoked in this way.

Counsel, please proceed. It is understood that these places were used for detention whatever their names. Do not dispute her.

In this way Judge Banda kept the air moving through the great bellows of the court.

Mataruga asked Esma, Could you leave the recreation hall?

No.

You did not go outside?

Yes, sometimes I hid in the bushes to avoid the soldiers. I am old. They were not looking for me.

Why did you not run away?

Esma said, Run where? We had nowhere to go. The town was occupied. We were starving. Where could we go without getting killed? I tried to get my granddaughter to come outside with me but she was too frightened. She thought they'd kill her.

How did you try to hide your granddaughter?

There was nowhere to hide. It is an empty hall. Only a bathroom at the back. I lay on top of her so if they were drunk they might not think of her. One night seven young girls were brought in with their mothers from a different village. They were too young and all of us fought the soldiers. But they hit us with their guns and their heavy boots. They knocked all of us out. When I revived, the girls were gone, my granddaughter too. Blood was everywhere. We tried to clean ourselves. But no water. The small children were crouching beside their unconscious mothers. Do not ever say ever again we are of the same fabric.

THE NIGHT BEFORE Edina testified, she telephoned me and said, From my hotel I can see the ocean.

I stepped out on my balcony and said, I am looking at the ocean too.

She said, A game?

You should sleep. Get rested for tomorrow.

Let's play. You take white, she said.

I set up my board quickly and said, e4.

d5, she said.

I took her pawn on d5. She moved her knight out, Nf6.

d4.

She said, Nxd5.

We played, c4 Nb4, then Qa4+ N8c6.

I heard her light a cigarette.

I asked, Are you ready? Is your mother all right? d5.

She said, b5. She is fine. Her assistant takes care of her. They try to avoid us being together so we don't talk about the trial.

I know, I said. Qxb5.

Then she made a cunning move, took her knight into my territory, Nc2+.

She said, I want it to be over. Do you listen to the news? They call us traumatized victims. What does the world know about the shattered insides of my body? I am no victim. Your turn.

Her knight perplexed me. I said, Kd1.

She liked that, said, Bd7.

I said, The world knows nothing. You will tell them.

I was already on the run. I said, dxc6.

Bg4 double check, she said.

I only had one move, king captures c2. I asked, What is your worst fear about tomorrow?

Edina played, Qd1 check. She said, I am afraid of seeing *him*. Your move.

Again, I could only see one move, Kc3.

She said, Qxc1+.

You have me, I said. I played, Kb3.

Edina said, Bd1+.

Damn, I said. I resign.

She laughed.

She seemed ready.

THE BLIND WAS down. On the other side of the glass he would be a few metres away from Edina. No filthy uniform. Hair still greasy. Even here. What did she smell? His sweat? Stale tobacco? Did she imagine the stench of alcohol on his breath and the smell of oil from his gun? She told me that sometimes the smells came back to her. She talked about his eyes.

I said, Don't look.

She said, I know.

I heard Karla begin. She showed Edina photographs of her hometown, her high school, the apartment where she grew up, the Partizan Sports Hall where she sang in school choirs and its small field where she played soccer as a girl. She identified the riverbank where Ivo first kissed her. She identified the mosque before it was blown up. She identified the Ribarski restaurant where Žarko sometimes rented her out. She identified the road to Miljevina, and to her grandmother's farm. She verified court charts with dates, and timelines of when they were taken to the Foča High School, to Partizan Sports Hall and to Karaman's house. She identified the Lepa Brena apartments, her childhood home and where she had been locked up waiting for men.

Karla showed Edina the list of witness names and numbers and asked her to verify where and when she had been with her mother, then her daughter. Dark stink. Crowded cars. Punching and forcing her through strange doorways. Memories must have pulled like quicksand but she kept answering in a clear and sure way. Then suddenly, not able to stop herself, she spoke of an incident she had forgotten until that moment in this powerful place of listening.

Edina said, In the spring Dragić moved me to a cottage. Soldiers came in and out and I had to cook for them and Dragić had his way with me and then gave me to other men.

This detail was not in her witness statement and Karla had never before heard it. Edina had not told it eight years ago. She had been ashamed. Never would she have wanted Ivo to know such a thing. She had forgotten it.

Karla revealed no surprise. Always new information is the danger with witnesses. She asked Edina to verify several easier facts. She would now have to map the new location and details of Dragić's movements. Joop was already writing notes.

She said, Please tell the court when you were separated from your family.

We were taken from our hiding place in a gully in the forest by men who were our *kums*.

Karla glanced up at the interpreters' booth and as soon as the interpretation was finished she said, Excuse me, Witness, for interrupting you. I just heard the interpreter say the word *neighbours* in English. But when you spoke you used the word *kum*. Will you explain to the court what *kum* means in your language?

Edina answered, This is a word for someone close. A godparent or a best man at a wedding. The parents of newlyweds call each other *kum*.

And so you knew the man who assaulted you?

Yes. It was a shock that a *kum* would hurt me.

What was the date?

I left home on June twenty-eighth. I remember because it was the holiday of Vidovdan. They probably didn't want to attack us on that day.

Edina had demonstrated an excellent memory.

She said, We were hiding in the forest and it was cold. I had a little radio and I was listening to news and when I heard gunshot from our village I woke people up and said, Let's move further away. The others were afraid to move. They said the dogs barking were wolves and then we heard a man shout, Catch them alive. Don't shoot. My mother told my father to run and he did and was shot before our eyes. Then my daughter and mother and three neighbours tried to hide. But a soldier, a neighbour I knew, shouted at us, Get out, *balijas,* a terrible word for Moslem. This is how he talked, swearing at us as if we were strangers. He had been my *kum*. He had eaten at my table.

Karla said, Thank you, Witness.

Judge Banda said, Recess.

Behind the glass and the blind I tried to absorb what I had heard. Beyond the pixelation and the altered witness voice and interpreter's neutral delivery and the time delay, it was still Edina.

—

THE NEXT MORNING Mataruga said to Edina, You have introduced a completely new event not in your previous statements. Could you tell us something about that?

About what?

That you went with Mr. Dragić to a mountain cabin.

I just remembered it.

So in fact you are giving us bit by bit what happened.

I am telling you everything I remember as I remember it.

When did you remember going there?

Yesterday.

I'm not asking you what you remembered yesterday, and don't look at the prosecution, please.

Why shouldn't I look at the prosecution?

Judge Banda urged, Counsel, go ahead with your questions. We are observing the witness here.

He said, Witness, I'm interested in knowing why you introduce new circumstances and new facts into the case.

Judge Banda said, Counsel, the witness has already explained that she gave explanations of the incidents as she remembered them.

Mataruga said, Your Honour, she responded that she decided to tell the truth when she came to court.

Ask her directly. I'm sure she has understood everything that you have said.

He turned back to Edina. Do I have to repeat the question or have you understood?

Repeat.

You said that you decided to tell the whole truth when you came before the Trial Chamber. This means that you did not tell the whole truth in your statements.

No, it does not mean that. Eight years ago, when I gave my first statement, I was ashamed and injured. I did not remember certain events. Now I remember more. Mr. Mataruga, I am an attorney. I know the importance of the whole truth. Perhaps you don't understand our language.

I do understand our language very well. But never mind. You said you stayed one night at a soldier's parents' house. He introduced you to his parents using a different name.

Where is your question? I had no choice. He said he would kill me. I had to meet his parents and pretend. He raped me on his childhood bed when the parents went out. Then other soldiers came in and they all raped me.

The gang rape, was it painful?

Yes.

How did this make you feel?

Dead.

Did you ever consider fleeing from the house?

How? There were soldiers everywhere. Every night they told us who they killed. They gave us their bloodstained uniforms to wash. They said no one would survive to tell the truth.

Did you see Mr. Dragić at the Lepa Brena apartments?

Yes, with PW-187.

How often?

Often. One time he had a car accident on the way and his ribs were damaged and I had to bandage him and he said, I wonder if you cast a curse on me. I thought, I would have cursed you with death, not a cracked rib.

Do not talk about made-up things like a curse.

He said the curse, not me.

How did you feel?

I was in a continual state of shock. Waiting to be raped or killed. How would you feel?

Your Honour, she asks questions.

Counsel, we are aware. Go ahead.

So you were living in an apartment with Mr. Dragić and his friends, cooking, washing, in fact keeping house for them. He tells the story differently. He claims he wanted to help you but you would not stop kissing him. That you took advantage of him.

He said I took advantage of him?

Witness, I must ask the questions. Did he try to help you?

Help me? He brought soldiers to rape me. Over and over he raped me and then he rejected me and took someone else.

What do you mean, he rejected you?

He did not want to rape me anymore. He gave me to someone else. They all took one girl after another.

Will you agree with me that when a person is jealous, she is ready to do certain things?

What are you talking about?

I'm referring to the fact that you said Dragić rejected you. In my understanding, when a man rejects a woman, it is someone he has loved. Perhaps you wanted to seduce him back?

Edina said nothing.

Mataruga said, Witness?

What?

Answer the question.

That is not a question. That is an evil lie.

Judge Banda interrupted. Counsel, after listening to the evidence and the witness's explanation and what she meant by the term *reject*, I don't think we should waste time. Please proceed with other questions.

Any of the judges could have reminded him that consent was not allowed as a defence because there can be no consent under conditions of slavery. This was clear in the rules. The defence lawyer ignored it. And in a momentary lapse, the others did not mention it.

I WAS ALONE that day in the gallery of Edina's cross and the questions were sickening. She was being assaulted again. She was lying under a giant ice pick and Mataruga was swinging and chopping down on her. Stop. Please. Stop battering her. Stop the lies. Once again she was alone and being assaulted.

She had to protect herself.

I heard her scrambled voice say under the neutral voice of the interpretation, Not even dead could I ever be Dragić's, or any one of theirs. Never. Not in all eternity.

She said deliberately, Put this on the record. Record this. Never, even dead, would I ever be one of theirs.

Judge Banda said, Don't bother, Witness. Don't waste your energy.

But Mataruga was permitted to finish his cross-examination.

Was Dragić at the school on January twenty-third?

I don't know.

At the Lepa Brena apartments on February third?

I don't know.

At the Partizan Sports Hall on March twelfth?

I don't know.

At Lepa Brena apartments April seventh to May twenty-first when forces were fighting in the western region?

She said, I don't remember.

I don't know.

I don't remember.

I cannot be sure who was there.

Edina blocked him. Both acted within the law. Like a king sliding in and out of check with no clear resolution.

I don't know.

I don't remember.

She could make Mataruga disappear the way she had made the rest of them disappear when they were hurting her.

The blows were still raining down on her. Where? When? Who? She resisted each blow. No answer. No answer. No answer.

He sat and watched. She told me that when she became disassociated in court and kept repeating the same answer she could see Dragić staring at her with a disgusting look of false tenderness as if he owned her and was sorry it had to be this way.

She said to Mataruga, Do *you* know where you were eight years ago? Do you think they gave us calendars?

Judge Banda said, Counsel, the witness does not know. Recess.

AFTER EDINA'S TESTIMONY, I wanted to go to her, but I could not. Her witness assistant took her back to the hotel, protected her from any contact.

Was this really the best we had, this bludgeon of law, the severed reality of the court? To extinguish rage as if it has no place in truth? To demean a woman? Make her a victim trying to defend herself all over again?

I went to the café in the Novotel next door, transcribed my notes, reread a letter from Mam. I wanted to call her and Biddy to hear their voices, but I did not trust myself not to cry. I looked at Mam's familiar handwriting. She had written that she had found a shoebox of old-fashioned christening announcements and antique funeral cards. She would keep for me the tattered notebook in which her grandmother had jotted entries about her eight children born one after another in a prairie farmhouse with a wood stove and no running water. She wrote, It is a good read. My grandfather wouldn't let her have the horses to drive to town when women first got the vote so she walked, thirteen miles in and thirteen miles back. And there is an entry after the flu death of her eldest son, Baden: *He's gone—my first baby— Tonight the sky feels too big—I am a speck—The stars are more real to me than anything down here—poor Baden—he always wanted to ride in an airplane—and now he never will.*

At the end of the letter Mam wrote that Biddy was doing well, becoming a young scientist. She wrote that the girl had taken to stargazing even in winter. She wrote, When the trial is over, I'm going on a holiday to Iceland to fly with some friends at their club. Work hard. Come home soon. XO, Mam.

DRAGIĆ STRUGGLED WITH the headphones and different languages. Did memories come back to him too, out of the fog of alcohol and the adrenalin of war? At Karaman's he had ordered the women to cook and serve him meat and fresh bread. Edina's was very good. He reported saying to her, I would come here only for your baking.

He made her serve it to him naked. He cracked her skull if he didn't like how she looked at him. He had said that he wanted her pregnant. He kept track of her in Foča, even when he was out dismantling booby traps and land mines.

MERIMA SPOKE CLEARLY and slowly. Many times she had rehearsed her story and she wanted to say it and go back to Vienna. She began, We girls were used as special rewards for soldiers. When Koza was finished with me, he let other men choose me. Sometimes they forced us to bathe them. They always kept their weapons with them. Sometimes they put guns under their pillows but I was too terrified to try to take one.

She told these details as if she were reciting. But already she had forgotten and called him Koza, his nickname. Why had she done this?

Karla asked, Can you identify in this courtroom a man who was there?

Yes. The man sitting two from the left, with a green stripe in his tie.

Do you know his name?

Žarko Dragić.

What was his nickname?

Koza.

What was his role?

He was the leader. The others obeyed him. At Ribarski restaurant he organized everyone for trading us.

Was he the first to rape you?

No, that was Stankić. He was our *kum* before. He was very forceful. He said he could have done worse but I was the same age as his daughter. He wanted to hurt me as much as possible. But he could never hurt me as much as my soul hurt me.

Did you tell your mother?

No. After I was taken away I did not see her again until after the war. For a long time I was afraid she was dead.

What about your grandmother?

No, I did not see her either. I thought she was dead.

How long were you there?

I don't know exactly. I know we were hiding on Vidovdan Day. Someone told me I was there for about eight months. I know when I left it was winter.

What did they do to you there?

They said we would have their babies. They said they would destroy us.

What did they do specifically to you?

They destroyed everything in me.

You were taken from Partizan Sports Hall by a group of men when you were hiding in the bathroom. Do you remember this night?

Yes. Because it was the first night. I remember most of their names because they often came for me later. Perhaps I will miss some because it has been eight years and I do not like to think about it. There was Luka Radović from Foča, Darko Dubljević, and Ranko Radulović, and Tolja and Bane. Those are nicknames, because I don't know their real names. Others I knew only their nicknames, Šćepo, Puko, Miga. There was one who had a wound in the stomach with a bandage, and they made me give him pleasure too, because he could not rape me with his wound.

These persons you mentioned, were they all soldiers?

Yes.

Who was their leader?

Koza, I mean that is the nickname for Dragić.

Where did they take you?

A motel in town, I do not remember the name.

How far was it from Partizan Sports Hall?

Not far, five minutes in their car.

And what did you do there?

They forced me to give them pleasure.

What do you mean by give them pleasure?

During the witness-proofing sessions, Merima had told Karla she had never wanted her mother and her grandmother to know the details of what had happened to her. She did not like to say the words in public. She was afraid when she saw him she would freeze inside.

Karla asked again, What do you mean by giving them pleasure?

I cannot express myself. Please, I cannot tell you this.

Please, just use the formal words. It is all right.

Even from behind the glass I could feel the stillness in the courtroom. She was again in the chaos and choking, covered with their filth. Darkness behind her eyes. Who in this courtroom knew what it was to be grabbed by men's hands, clothes stripped off, burned with a cigarette on her nipple? Who had heard themselves scream?

She had tried to forget about it in Vienna. And these lawyers arrived and disturbed her peace.

he pointed his finger and chose me they were all drunk and stinking I was fighting them and there was the cold blade of a knife against my cheek a man is behind holding my wrists and a man is in front ripping off my clothes, putting his face on my face, breath-stink and I am naked, they tore away my clothes and opened their rough pants and now my shoulders are jerked and my hands are grabbed by one on each side, everything happening all at once, I am not me, a man is kneeling over me and squeezing my jaw open and putting it in, his thing in my mouth and down my throat and I am choking and another is pushing my legs apart and jamming himself inside and one of them has cracked my knuckles with a gun butt and he is putting it in my hand and on the other side too and stick is all over my arms and face and lips and legs and they are on me like a pack of wild animals, changing places and I cannot see who is where, I am just trying to get my breath and finally they are finished and I am lying alone and they are zipping and reaching for cigarettes and matches and now one of them has grabbed my wrist and jerked me up and I have trouble to stand

Karla repeated, Please, we need you to tell us exactly what happened. Just use correct language. Did you have a penis in your mouth?

Yes.

What else? Please just describe.

I cannot say.

Please try.

Try.

They came in together and all got on me at the same time.

How many?

Five.

Where were they on your body?

I can't say.

Just use formal words.

Say it.

145

One in the mouth, one down below, one in each hand.

That is four.

There were five. I think they took turns below.

How long did this go on?

It has never stopped.

I don't remember. An hour? It felt long.

What happened when it was over?

I was destroyed.

They left. I went to the bathroom for water. A young one came in, Tolja. He tried to give me a hand grenade. He said, They might cut your breasts. Please, if they want to cut you up, pull this pin. You will be gone, but quite a few of them will be gone too. I was too afraid to take it. One came in with a knife and he said, Which breast do you like better? But Tolja stood over me and said, Please don't do anything to her. She's such a wonderful girl. So the one with the knife spat at him and called him a name and then he raped me again and then a commander walked in and he stopped. That is all I can remember.

Karla asked Merima, What happened after?

The next day they took me back to Partizan.

What did you do there?

I hid under my grandmother.

Judge Banda interrupted, Counsel, break.

A WOMAN CAN disappear, like the girls in old fairy tales who disappear into forests. She leaves home behind and goes to a new place. She becomes a creature who escapes a curse or a demon or a wicked stepmother. She hides and is tricked into revealing herself. Glass slippers. Coats of fur. Riddles.

In the old fairy tales girls escape from one kingdom only to end up in a different and not necessarily better kingdom. A girl gets absorbed into other people's stories. She doesn't go home. She carries her home inside her. A woman must make her home wherever she is. This must be her happily-ever-after. Esma and Merima would never go home. The homes they carried inside were now in a foreign place.

In the gallery, I used coloured tabs in my notebooks to help me remember the details of each woman's testimony: *Who* was yellow. *What*, red. *Where*, green. *When*, blue. There was no *Why*.

MATARUGA ROSE TO cross-examine Merima. He asked about places and dates. Over and over she said she did not know.

The lawyer said, You remember only for the prosecution.

He opened his hands toward the judges, as if he were helpless and wronged.

Karla stood for the last time with Merima and asked, Witness, for identification purposes, is there anything characteristic about Mr. Dragić to make clear to the court who he is?

Yes.

Karla hoped she would say the scar on his cheek.

Tell us what that was.

The eyes. Never will I forget his eyes.

FIFTY-ONE MORE COURT days from March to November, thirteen more women witnesses for the prosecution, to be followed by expert witnesses for both sides. Military witnesses spoke to the hierarchies of command and to more history.

The judges asked witnesses to refrain from beginning with the Ottomans. There were no female military or expert witnesses. The case dragged on. Intricacies of law were combed out, like untangling strand by strand the fine horsehair for the bow of the violin. Which story exactly matched definitions of genocide, crimes against humanity, enslavement?

I often watched the Dutch guard, Lieven, in court beside Dragić. We had met in a café near the courts and he said he had seen me every day in the gallery. One night we went to my apartment. Expat life is lonely. He was the sort of man who loves a woman's pleasure as much as his own. I did not analyze it much. Everyone who worked in the courts was transient. Desire is as ungovernable as air. I did not want to spoil my nights with Lieven by thinking too much about them. Lieven guarded the accused, watched him pick his cuticles, was alert to his tiniest physical movements, and that was all.

In court, Lieven's face was still, professional. If the blind was up, he sometimes glanced at me and I noticed a delicate flush on his jawline.

In my apartment I asked, What do you talk about while he's smoking during the breaks?

Nothing. I don't know his language.

Why don't you wear headphones in court?

It is not my job to follow the proceedings.

But he might do something, strangle his attorney, take poison.

Lieven shook his head. He said, That cannot happen. It is why I am there.

But what if something happens during the proceedings? Don't you want to know?

Lieven reached for the buttons on my blouse and said, I am good at my job.

He slipped my blouse off.

I said, I see you from the gallery. What do you think about when you're guarding?

You.

That's not true. Do you have other girlfriends?

Wat ben je toch een lekker ding.

I understood only the word for delicious so I let it go. We were just two people who worked in the same building. When you work closely with people, you sleep with them from time to time, you just do, you need to, and this revives you like a sip of spring water.

TWO EXPERT WITNESSES cancelled after listening to the televised proceedings. The judges chided lawyers for delays, for scheduling gaps. Karla and her team continued to weave individual testimonies into a collective story, each voice substantiating the others, to demonstrate systematic intent. They corroborated dates. Nura Muslimović, PW-91, remembered the day she was taken away from her village because it was her mother's birthday. PW-75, Šefika Tvrtković, remembered the day her daughter was taken because it was St. Ilija's Day, a holiday for all her village though the Serbs call it Ilinden and Muslims call it Alidjun. Mothers marked their time by their children. Mubera Sokolović, PW-187, said, I was there for six months. I know because I wanted to know how my pregnancy was advancing. When the security officers at the doors had newspapers I borrowed them and checked the dates. Anyway I lost the baby at four months and seven days and I am glad. I will never bring a child into this world. Never. The soldiers made us monsters. One night I saved myself by picking up a baby and making it scream when a soldier was dragging me to the door. He threw me off him and said, Not you, I'm not listening to a screaming baby. I was shocked at myself that I did this and I never did it again. Nejra Kulenović, PW-186, was the mother of that baby. Her two children were with her in Partizan, two years old and ten months. She was determined to remember her children's milestones, first steps and words, and she scratched little marks in the bathroom which the investigators documented. Her milk dried up. She was continuously taken away by groups of soldiers for an hour, a day, three days, and each time she was pushed back into the hall she looked only for her children.

She testified, When I came back I tried to hide my burns, bruises. But I counted days. To know their ages.

The interpreters never interrupted the women witnesses or asked them to slow down. The rhythm of emotion is uneven. Rage and indignation can be told from a tightened throat or in open sobbing. Some of the interpreters unconsciously mirrored the women's rhythms.

Breath, like the eyes, cannot be rendered emotionless.

FINALLY. THE DAY of the last prosecution witness.

Jasmina Begović, PW-52.

The blind was up for her because she was the mother of a girl who was never found. She wanted to testify in open court. She wanted her daughter's name not to be forgotten.

Karla had scheduled her last because her testimony was meant to linger in the judges' minds. As she had earlier agreed, William Steyn was assigned to question her.

Jasmina had managed to hide her twelve-year-old daughter, Hana, from the soldiers by keeping her with very small children. After six dreadful weeks, on the day that group of mothers and babies and small children were being moved to Tuzla, their bus was stopped on the bridge on the way out of town. A soldier saw Hana and pulled her out of the bus. Jasmina was screaming and holding on to her child and the soldier knocked her out with the butt of his rifle. PW-31 and PW-97 verified the girl was taken from the bus, and Edina had earlier verified she was brought to Karaman's house, where Edina often tried to hide her. One night the soldiers came in late and Edina hid the child under the bed and when they were gone, she found the little girl curled like a snail under an old potato bag. Hana used to bring in a bit of mint from outside to sniff. Later PW-199 saw her being sold to a soldier in the Ribarski restaurant.

The prosecution scheduled an afternoon session with Hana's mother, hoping her cross-examination would take place in the morning, after she had rested. During the witness-proofing, Steyn told her he would show her a picture to verify her daughter's identity. Then she would be asked to describe the child's disappearance.

In court he handed Jasmina the photo of Hana.

She looked down at the familiar picture. Here, under the eyes of the judges, she saw it fresh. Look, her small girl was alive, there, oh, her trusting eyes shining, her sweet lips. She could smell Hana's fresh skin after playing outside on the mountain. Look, the little front curl of hair slipping loose.

Tonight she'll kiss her goodnight and lie down beside her until she falls asleep.

Jasmina was wearing a bit of Hana's hair in a locket a neighbour had found in the burned rubble of her house. Hana would have been twenty years old. Everyone in the court was waiting to begin after the simple identification.

Jasmina opened her mouth to say yes but a different sound was coming out, a crying moan like a half-alive creature in the mouth of a snake. Swallow, die more, swallow, die. She was a creature in hell, frozen on one side, burning on the other.

From the gallery I saw the back of the mother bent over a photograph. Never had I heard such a cry from a human being. The courtroom fell still.

I looked up to the interpreters' booth where they waited, no translation possible.

After a long, long time Jasmina had to breathe, and she looked around as if the sound had come from someone else. William Steyn stepped between her and Dragić to try to block her view of him. Judge Banda tipped her chin down toward the witness as if ready to call a break.

Then Jasmina looked up into Judge Banda's eyes and spoke, That is my daughter. Hana.

AT THE RECESS I had to get out. I went to the Mauritshuis gallery, a half-hour walk from the courts. I did not want to be alone. I often went to that gallery because I like the art of the Golden Age, the radiance in the paint, Protestant wives who tucked their hair under scarves and hats and plucked chickens in kitchens and lice from each other's hair and men who played lutes. Warm domestic scenes. Beyond the walls of their homes were the bloody battles of the Reformation. We could not guess from those domestic paintings that in the Battle of White Mountain four thousand Bohemian Protestants were killed in one hour.

I stopped in front of a painting of a woman in a white smock worn over full blue-green skirts, her feet on a warming block. In the large canvas, she is bent over her sewing. A man stands with his hand on her right shoulder and he is twisted over her, his open left palm thrusting coins at her. Her eyes are fixed on her needlework but she is awkwardly turned away and acutely aware of him and the insistent pressure of his fingers on her flesh.

I was startled to hear a Dutch woman beside me say in English, It is a remarkable painting. Judith Leyster painted it when she was twenty-two years old.

Hmmm, I said.

She painted only six years, said the woman. And then she married a painter and had five children. She may have painted in her husband's atelier. This was common but we do not know.

I nodded.

We almost lost her. Her signature was *JL* with a star. Franz Hals stole her paintings and painted his signature over hers and showed them as his own. The fraud lasted for three hundred years. Finally someone with sharp eyes at the Louvre detected something in the style.

I could smell coffee on her breath. The room felt close and threatening. I had to get out before the man in the painting made her drop her sewing. His eyes were piercing. She was trapped.

I turned away from the woman and she leaned in and said, You know, in Dutch our word for sewing is slang for sex.

I escaped to the cobbled courtyard, walked quickly through the iron gates and onto the street. I had to clear my head. I thought, What is wrong? Strangers discuss paintings all the time. I thought, This trial will not let women's lives be painted over and lost.

WHEN COURT RESUMED in the afternoon, Karla's lips were pressed tight, deepening a dimple that was in no way cheerful. As she listened to Steyn question Hana's mother, I watched her shift slightly forward. She could do nothing. No one had anticipated the mother's unearthly cry.

Steyn needed Jasmina to speak, not to publicly mourn. And so he pressed on. When did she last see her child? Where? Who took her from the bus when they were leaving town? Was she ever found? He needed the mother to describe how her wisp of a child's body had been made a battlefield on which large, uniformed, armed and brutal men fought.

After Jasmina's testimony, I called Edina.

Kosmos answered, We're having a joint.

I said to Edina, Did you know Jasmina's daughter?

Hana, she said. She was the flower girl at our wedding.

She was at Karaman's house with you?

Yes.

I heard Kosmos stand and walk across the room and say, Forgive us all.

Edina? I said.

She said quietly, They wanted to hurt us like it was their job. Hana stopped screaming. She was so small. What did they see when they looked at her? They hurt us because they could. Night after night they performed for each other. Animals. They brought young men and forced them. We were furniture. She was a little girl. How could they? I am two people, the person before and the person after. Better to be dead.

I GOT A toothache while I was in The Hague and when the dentist came in, my knuckles were white from grasping the chair and he said, We must postpone to another day. I think you are not well.

I went to the cinema and sat alone and when someone tried to go past me I refused and waved them to a different row. It was intolerable to be near a stranger in the dark.

I bought small Delft night lights in the shapes of canal houses and tulips for my apartment. I saved the largest, a cheery blue teapot, to illuminate my bedroom.

But darkness seeped through. History is not scattered ashes. History is now. The women were made less than human because of being in a particular moment of history. Through no fault of their own. People claimed not to know. The women's stories were denied. *You don't want to listen? Listen anyhow.*

OVER THE MONTHS of the trial, Karla and Andro and William developed an affectionate relationship, enjoyed opera together. I saw them once in Amsterdam at *Lucia di Lammermoor*. After the trial Karla told me about a turning point in their reasoning that may have come during one of their social times. She said that William had learned to appreciate her relationship with the women witnesses, and had told her that she provoked him to think in new ways. She said, He was not only collegial but sought friendship too which I liked. He shared my ambition in this case.

She said, We both feared the court would not decide to place the rapes within a larger program of ethnic cleansing. It was a difficult legal bar to meet. We struggled to prove intention.

Here was the problem, she said. Our case was focused uniquely on Foča even though rape had happened throughout the region. Because of this it was still *possible* to see the rapes as the depravity of individual men in one place and not as part of a widespread genocidal campaign. As the trial progressed, we sometimes had a cup of coffee together before going home. One of these times, William confessed to me that he was racking his brains trying to figure out what would meet the standard of widespread and systematic attacks on civilians.

I told him I'd never been exactly sure of the meaning of this English phrase, racking the brains.

I liked to tease him about language but he was not very accustomed to language play. So he answered seriously, It means tortured stretching.

I laughed and told him that it was exactly what I too had been suffering.

I told him that in the Srebrenica trial that was being conducted at the same time, patterns were becoming clear to me. There were three tactics in ethnic cleansing: kill a portion of people, beat a portion of people and rape the women. Life becomes so unbearable that anyone alive tries to escape. The intended result is that all the people leave.

William said, And so, in Foča, we know men were murdered, others were beaten and the women were raped over and over. In a single year, the entire Moslem population of the town was murdered, imprisoned or left.

Suddenly, from our refined articulation of the pattern, a new pattern appeared. It was our epiphany moment in this trial when, aha! we saw what we had been searching for.

We could finally see that the rape camps—throughout the region—were part of widespread and systematic attacks on civilians, and were not just the idiosyncratic behaviour of a few men in Foča.

We had finally stepped back together to see the larger picture. We had finally articulated a pattern that now appeared obvious. Rape was not about war booty or spoils. Rape was part of a widespread attack meant to result in the extermination of a people. Ethnic cleansing. It seems so obvious now. But for us at the time it was a consciousness shift. A new idea. And so obvious that we were certain we could make it hold up.

The law seeks truth but it does not define truth. People define truth. Now we had to take this truth to court.

I OFTEN MADE sketches of Dragić's eyes. The eyelids drooped, as if he could doze with his eyes open, like a bored boy at the back of the classroom. When he was called to speak, his eyes were unnaturally open, two burning stones in bloodshot snow. He only relaxed when he spoke about military leadership. His eyes knew how to adjust to mountain darkness and how to threaten men into submission.

Lieven told me Dragić had no friends in the detention centre. He lifted weights and watched television. Of course he did not fit in with the generals and politicians. I asked what else there was to do. Lieven said some detainees liked working with clay and made primitive figurines of animals and roses. But not Dragić.

Lieven said, You do not have to worry about what they do.

He put his hands around my waist and I asked, But does he talk with no one?

He likes to smoke. I'm not supposed to talk about these things, especially to the media.

I am not media.

You will write about this trial. It is why you are here. Your friend does little, Goat, lies on his bed. He is a *woesteling*.

What's that?

A criminal, you know, like a low form of man, a beast.

I asked how a man could want to hurt a woman with his own body in this way.

Lieven said, You do not ask the right question. A soldier only sees an enemy.

A beast, I said. Not human. Do you think Dragić would rape again?

Lieven got impatient then, said, He is a man at war inside himself. He won't have a chance again. I am not going to waste my time at night thinking about him. I have to guard him all day.

War makes murderers of ordinary men.

Not all men. He is a brute. War took away constraints and he found none inside himself. Are you tired of talking yet?

Yes.

Is this okay? he asked as he unbuttoned my blouse.

Yes.

He said, Your questions are sad and strange.

—

WILLIAM STEYN WAS on his feet again. He moved with ease, his body concentrated but relaxed, and he appeared to enjoy the performance part of a trial. He was one of those rare mature men blessed with confidence. He was here because he wanted to do something meaningful. Later I read that he was the first in his immigrant family to be educated. He had grown bored, wanted the stimulation of being in a world court, wanted to work with new people from many legal traditions. Back at home his neglected marriage was over. His children grown. And here he loved the new challenges and the high stakes.

They had been questioning a military historian, and near the end of his cross-questioning, Judge Romano asked Steyn to make a connection between a campaign of ethnic cleansing, which Mr. Dragić claimed he was unaware of, and the particular crime of rape.

Romano had rarely spoken during all the months of proceedings. I put down my sketching and listened carefully.

Steyn responded, The court has heard from three generations of women in the same family. This illustrates an attempt to destroy the past, present and future of a community and ultimately, a population.

He reiterated that the court had heard from witnesses about a single man. He reminded the court of the thousands of pages of written statements submitted from victims throughout the region who had not been brought to testify.

Judge Romano, who had much more experience in this international court than most of the lawyers, pointed out that Article 5 did not require the prosecution to prove that the rapes were widespread but to prove that armed conflict against the civilian population was widespread.

Steyn and Karla had discussed this over and over as they looked for the connections.

Steyn answered, Absolutely. Rape is a constituent element in the widespread or systematic attack against civilians meant to destroy a people.

All three judges, Romano, Smith and Banda, saw the connection.

With these words, the law could change.

An individual woman was no longer a spoil of war.

Monumental jurisprudence. A new way of thinking. Nine months of exploring the way the rapes had taken place and the effects of those rapes had shown that rape is an attack on human dignity. Sexual integrity and human dignity are too tightly intertwined to be separable. To violate one violates the other. Rape is an attack on our shared human condition. A crime against humanity.

I watched Steyn sit down and raise his eyebrows to share the moment of victory with Karla. In this brief and complex moment their team had not fallen short.

THE CORNERSTONE OF the defence lawyer's strategy had been that Dragić had no authority over the men in his unit once they had returned to Foča from active duty. In this way, the assaults in town could not be considered systematic or widespread. They were the chaotic actions of depraved men. Mataruga brought in a retired general, now a professor, and for three days the general argued that command responsibility is only when men are *functionally* engaged in a mission. For three days he also said that the interpreters were not doing a good job and confused the interpretations of the words for command and direction and control, *komandovanje, rukovodjenje* and *kontrola*. I looked up to see the usually cool-headed professionals in the interpreters' booth occasionally tighten their lips at his accusations.

ON THE LAST scheduled day with the general, William and Karla decided to question him together, hoping he would underestimate a woman. William began in the morning.

General, he said, do military regulations state that the responsibility of a commander includes the conduct of his subordinates?

Yes.

The regulations say that this includes undertaking all the necessary steps to prevent the perpetration of war crimes or crimes against humanity?

Yes, yes.

Professor, are there any exceptions?

No.

Can you point to any section in the regulations that says functional commanders are not responsible for the actions of their subordinates?

I cannot point to that. But the fine point is that the responsibility is temporary because the group itself is temporary. And the Foča units were informal.

In the afternoon, Karla picked up the questioning.

She said, General, the accused said, quote, *I lined up my men and told them whoever raped one of the women I was personally going to execute them*. This is consistent with someone who is in charge. In another part of his statement he said, quote, *I issued him an order to not let anyone in the house.* Is this not the clear language of someone in charge?

The general responded, You interpret it that way. I interpret it as a man protecting his reputation.

Karla said, The men obeyed the order. Would you agree the men believed he was their commander?

It does not seem that way to me.

Karla pressed, So, the men follow his orders while they are on military missions together because he is their commander. Back from their assignments, the group is disbanded and they are not under his command. But he orders them to guard the door of a house where women are being raped and they obey.

She moved to the general's left side. She had noticed when William was questioning that the general was agitated by this and she learned that he had no peripheral vision in his left eye, a war wound.

Karla moved in and out of his vision, said, And if the accused posted a guard on the door, does this not suggest he knew someone inside needed protection?

No, it does not.

Then what does it suggest?

They would not know what was going on inside. They were just doing what they were told.

Obeying orders?

Karla glanced at William. *Boxed in.*

AFTER MAKING LOVE, the eyes are soft, the jawline soft. I love the delicate colour under the cheeks. I love the human face. Day after day for weeks, when the blind was down in the gallery, I listened to the voices of the interpreters and tried to imagine the faces of the women who spoke.

Now the blind was up. I watched the strained tilt of Dragić's head to the right become more pronounced, and the deepening crease between the eyebrows and the jaw clenched hard. His head was balding below the crown and his hair loss had quickened. I saw a new anxiousness in a twitch in his left eye and though I could not see his feet, his continuous restless shifting seemed to begin in his legs. He often dipped his chin and turned his head to stretch the sides of his neck. Stillness made him wary. Sometimes I imagined him on the mountain, prowling through darkness, alert to the broken twig revealing the hidden mine. He would no doubt perceive odd movements in half-light and hear sounds others did not. His men depended on his senses to keep them alive. On the mountain he was a skilled survivor.

Here, in the court, he was expert in nothing, a nearly illiterate unofficial soldier. He continually opened his mouth and rubbed his tongue over a back tooth. I watched the delayed television transmissions and saw how his eyes widened revealing the whites all around, the pupils dilated, his expression defensive and wild.

Steyn questioned Dragić about Edina.

He said, She kissed me, and I tried to refuse her behaviour but she put her hand on my mouth.

Steyn said, You are strong. You could have stopped her.

She kept kissing me, Dragić said. She would not allow me to talk. She looked like a vegetable because the others did so many things to her. How could I be attracted? I claim this as truth that she fondled me, for ten, fifteen minutes, and did everything to excite my manhood. So I followed through.

He spoke with quickened breath and his skin coloured under his cheeks and his hand constantly worried his eye. I listened to his unbelievable fantasy about Edina. Dragić could not make me believe in even a few minutes of his life. Because storytellers believe in their dragons and glass slippers, they can make their listeners believe. But Dragić did not believe in his own lies and he could not make any of us believe either.

Judge Banda asked, Is it your position PW-71 seduced you?

He answered, I had sexual intercourse with her against my will. I did not want to, you know how it is.

Judge Banda interrupted him, That's enough. Questions, please.

Steyn said, The court has heard PW-71's testimony. Beatings, starvation, humiliation, fear for her life. The accused is trying to tell us that the victim raped him. No, Your Honour, I have no questions.

IN HIS CLOSING statement, Steyn spoke to the honesty of the women and to the sincerity of their emotions. They had travelled to the court and they had told about the things that happened to them for which there are no easy words. He reminded the judges that though they had been incarcerated and starved and beaten and assaulted, they also mentioned in their testimonies small kindnesses from certain people, a bit of offered food, a moment of protection. He said that this showed how the women did not come for revenge but to tell their full experience, to truthfully bear witness.

Behind the glass I listened and watched. Each woman had told things they wanted to forget and each suffered shame. Each woman had reached inside for strength to speak. But strength does not sweep away anguish and fear.

The women were not human to Dragić. He claimed that he

was only doing what everyone did. There were thousands of men like him. What is the absence of empathy for another? I do not know but I do know that violence and cruelty step into this absence. It can happen anywhere. Some of the women felt that the trial was like washing a mortal wound—it did neither good nor harm. The wound would still be mortal. And yet still they spoke.

I WENT HOME at the end of November to wait for the judgment. I did not easily fit back into my old life in Toronto. The city felt grey, dull. People felt dull. I walked by the grey lake. I visited Jacques Payac who was finishing an edit on green technologies and he did not have time to talk and told me to come back in a few days. I was an outsider at home. I made myself fit into Mam's and Biddy's peaceful routines. Biddy asked if I had seen her father and when would she meet him.

I said, Soon now. This summer.

She asked again for stories about him and what he was like and if he had changed and where did he live and what did he do and when she would go. She said, Will I have grandparents there? Cousins? I had to tell her that the war had created great loss in his life. She thought this over and I saw her put a few more of her hopes aside. She seemed very alone.

I asked, What do you hope for most when you see him?

She said, I want to know if he loves me. I want to know why he left.

BIDDY WAS RUNNING her school's science fair and she had recreated a Michelson interferometer with mirrors and a laser pointer and some little mounts and a ruler and Post-it notes. She explained how she measured the wavelength of optical beams, that the tool was used to detect gravitational waves. Her deft hands adjusted the lenses and her fingers pointed to light sources. I could not follow the calculations.

She said, Don't worry. Mam can't either.

She was proud to have knowledge I did not.

We looked at an incubator she had set up in the living room.

Hatching eggs?

Biddy said, My friend can't have it at home because her mother doesn't want a bunch of Rhode Island Reds running around the house.

Mam said, I can't say I blame her. We haven't figured out what to do with the chicks after the science fair.

Biddy and her friend Emily often sat together staring at the eggs. One evening Biddy knelt with her lips pressed against the glass while I was reading.

I asked, What are you doing?

I'm thinking about the eggs.

What are you thinking?

I'm thinking about the yolk becoming the embryo and the heart and the blood vessels and the tail bud and the wing and leg buds, the brain and eyes.

She showed me Emily's charts, coloured pictures of chick development. Each egg was numbered.

Why did Emily number the eggs?

Biddy said, It's an *experiment*.

On the twenty-first day the girls stayed home from school to watch. We called Mam to come but she said she would leave all that birthing in their capable hands. She was going to the airfield.

In the evening we finally heard a wobbling as the eggs shook back and forth and then the first pipping of the egg tooth as the little chicks broke through the shells. Biddy had predicted numbers 9, 3 and 6 would hatch first and they did in that order. Emily had worried along with Biddy about number 11 and indeed it never hatched. The chick was turned over inside and drowned. The two girls put the eleven surviving chicks in a box they had prepared with warming lights and took the drowned bird outside in the dark to bury near Biddy's previous pets, a goldfish and a hamster.

I asked Biddy, How did you know which would hatch first? She said, I watched them.

Emily said, They really give birth to themselves. They just peck their way out when they are ready.

I said, I would like to do this.

Emily said, But you're already born.

I know, I said. But maybe we are born over and over. Maybe we need to keep pecking ourselves out.

Biddy said to Emily, She always talks like that. It isn't very scientific.

Emily said to me, You would have to be careful not to get turned over and drown.

I WAS HAPPY to be back in The Hague.

I walked through a city that was now stitched into me. I walked through the Peace Palace and saw again the Japanese gobelins and remembered my hours in the library. I walked on the beach. I heard that Lise was leaving the court. That she had a job as a secretary. After her brilliant fieldwork with the women, making the first approaches, creating the relationships for Karla and the rest

of the team, working on the trial, she had tried to keep her professional reserve but the stories haunted her, and the suffering broke
her. Karla asked her if she could find the right armour to put on to
keep working, but Lise simply said, I need to get out. All of us who
interpret are damaged to some degree.

One evening I was in an Aldi to pick up something for breakfast and a stranger approached me where I stood in front of the
large refrigerators.

The woman said, I am supposed to testify tomorrow.

Oh, I said.

You were watching the trials. I saw you there.

Yes, I said. They will read the Foča judgment tomorrow. That
is what I'm here for.

I am afraid I will not be able to bring myself to speak in court.

I said, I am sorry. It is very difficult.

Why are you here?

I have a friend who testified.

Quite spontaneously, in the way we sometimes tell strangers
intimate details of our lives, I told her the truth. I told her I had
been drawn to watch these trials because of this friendship, but
also because I knew a man from the region, and I watched the
war on television and I could no longer remain indifferent. I said
that I had learned that we revolt when something threatens our
inner meaning. That watching this war had touched something
inviolable in me, and I could no longer turn away.

I said, I know nothing of what it is to be in war. But you do.
If I do not listen to you, who am I?

The woman traced her finger nervously along the cold shelf.
She said, I cannot bear to say what happened to me during the
war. I hate my own voice, the tissue in my own throat. Can you

imagine? Horrible. Horrible. I will be silent to death. I will not be a victim.

Neither of us was choosing cheese or milk or anything from the refrigerated shelves. I said, I like your voice. I don't think you are a victim. You are the strong one.

Unexpectedly she laughed. She said, I am not strong. In my town is a memorial stone to all those killed soldiers. Is there anything for me? No. There is no stone inscribed: *Remember all the heroic women raped in this place for nothing.*

Then she chose a single small container of Fage plain yogurt off the shelf and looked at it as if it were something unknown to her.

THE LAW CREATES a scaffold of order and civility. But every person who has been through a trial knows that under the surface lie cruelties. We accept law's illusions because we have nothing better. We try to shape our complicated ideas into acts. It is all we can do. We are otherwise creatures driven by rage and revenge.

Judge Gladys Banda today would read the long judgment. She and Smith and Romano had had long discussions, reviewed thousands of pages of evidence and testimony in order to write the three-hundred-page judgment. The women witnesses had spoken. *I feel dead but I am condemned to live. I feel destroyed.* These words would have settled in Gladys Banda in a place she could not completely cordon off. All her life she had fought the idea of women as property and so, legitimate spoils of war. This judgment would find rape in war to be an assault on human dignity.

But today, when Judge Banda read the court's carefully written decision aloud to the world, she would also read it to an individual man. She would say to him, *You were a courageous soldier and your men indisputably held you in high esteem. By your natural authority you could easily have put an end to these women's suffering. Your active participation in this nightmarish sexual exploitation is therefore even more repugnant. You thrived in the dark atmosphere of dehumanizing others.*

How does a judge feel on the morning of a judgment? Today's judgment would irrevocably change a single man's life. He would go to a foreign prison far from home. He had behaved as thousands did during the war but *this* man, today, would be condemned to spend the next twenty-eight years of his life in prison.

Today Judge Gladys Banda would get out of bed, eat breakfast, put on her coat, wish her family a good day, close the door of her apartment and come to the court. Today the law would change. And a man's life. And perhaps the women's lives. Of this she could not be sure. In what way did she clear her mind? Did she take a coffee on the way? Did she pray?

I TELEPHONED KOSMOS and Edina and asked if they were going to watch the judgment. Kosmos said, Yes. The actors want their stage back, so it is our last day here. They want to even throw out our chairs. I told them to go away for a few more hours and the director complained and I said, *Poserem ti se u ruku, pa nosi.*

I was laughing but I did not know what it meant.

What did you say?

I can't translate, said Kosmos. But he shouted to people

behind him, *Sisaj mi pitona*, and to me, I told them to suck my you-know-what.

Python? I said. Always he made me laugh.

Then he said, I brought vodka for Edina to drink.

I said, I wish I was with you both.

Yes, he said. I am mixing it with tomato juice and Tabasco.

A Bloody Mary, I said.

Yes, he said. I learned this uncivilized drink from a Canadian actor in London. But I do it my own way.

How?

I have the bullet that shot my grandfather's shoulder in *his* war. I open it and put a few grains of gunpowder into the drink. This makes it a Bloody Bosnian.

Tell Edina I am thinking of her, I said.

THROUGH THE GLASS, I watched Dragić's jaw clench and unclench as he stood to hear the verdict. First he had to wait for the interpretation. When the sentence reached him, he shook his head. Wronged.

Mataruga leaned in, no doubt to tell him they would appeal. I watched the man absorb, with shock, with anger, what had really taken place in the last eight months. He was going to prison. He knew that others from the detention centre were imprisoned in Norway and Sweden and Germany and Italy. I had heard that Dragić had had death threats from men he had named in his old unit. He could not even go home safely. I watched the white knuckles of his clasped hands and the disbelief in his shoulders.

—

AFTERWARDS EDINA WOULD not pick up the telephone. Kosmos said they smoked and drank their gunpowder vodka.

Kosmos told me that when he said *You won* and got up to hug Edina she moved away from him. So he unplugged the television and wound the extension cord around his open hand and his elbow and asked her, What now?

Work. You?

Kosmos said, I told her I will write my play about bridges.

IT WAS THE women witnesses who won this case. They refused to back down and they refused to remain silent and they refused to hide. They transmuted the word *victim* into *hero*. I am in awe of their strength. They spoke. For themselves, and for us. The whole world cannot stand trial. But we can all be responsible. A human is human through others.

Sarajevo, Toronto

I FLEW TO Sarajevo.

Edina slept a lot, woke up, played chess with me and slept again. Said she needed to work. Said they needed trials here now. Said thousands of men who had committed the same terrible crimes sat in cafés drinking coffee.

She said, It was a letdown. Was it not a letdown?

I said, You changed the law.

I found Kosmos in the theatre and we made love in the projection booth while the movie was playing. I said, Aren't you afraid someone will hear us?

No, he said.

During the last reel as we rested on his mattress on the floor watching the flickering light, he spoke about his family. He said, I lost them all. My brother. What do trials do?

We listened to the *ticka-ticka* of the projector. He was alone lying in my arms that day. We were amphibious creatures at the bottom of the sea looking up through fathoms of water, his dear voice describing all the ocean's loved and lost.

He said, Now you will not be in Europe so often.

I will still visit and you can come to Toronto.

He said, I waited for a long time to come back to my fucked-up city and I like it here. Maybe one trip to Toronto before we all die.

I said, You need to come.

Then I laughed, I will buy a burial plot for three, for you and Edina and me.

He said, We will always be together.

Where shall I buy the plot? I asked. No one dies where they are born.

I want to, he said.

I said, She loved Ivan. We need a plot for him too.

He's buried already, said Kosmos. You too are becoming end-of-the-earth crazy.

Are you sure you don't want to come home with me?

I am sure.

What about our daughter?

Bring her here. I will show her the kapia on the bridge over the river Drina.

She will love you.

I know, he said.

She needs to know you.

She is almost grown up, he said.

She still needs you. So her pain does not go into the next generation.

I SAW MAK with his two sons and their girlfriends in a café in the old town and he called over loudly and I waved to him but did not want to join him. He got up anyway and came over and said, You no good? What is happening?

And I said, It is nothing. It is only the trial. But it is over now.

I loved the stoop in Mak's shoulders and how he leaned his ear toward me. With one arm he hugged me and said, War is never over. When I am dying I will cry out about the war. I have seen old soldiers do this. Put aside sadness. What is that word in English meaning do something to make past better?

A trial?

No, more like spiritual.

Redeem?

Yes. Live, he said. Redeem.

I SLEPT AT Edina's apartment, brought in food and wine and cigarettes.

She said, A trial changes a person. Have you written anything yet?

I'm working on it.

You have been thinking about this for a long time.

I know.

She said, Your writing is like the bridge in Jablanica. Do you know it?

No.

Never mind. Let's play.

We set up the board but after only a dozen moves she said, You still play like a chess tourist.

I laughed, Can't help it. I get distracted.

You should study more.

I know.

I pretended to be upset. Through her window I could see the mountain and the first grey in the blackness and the stars fading, only Venus still bright and low. I wanted to sleep. But she poured us a glass of slivovitz and said, There is something I want to tell you.

She was wrapped in an old blanket. Her cigarettes were on the frayed arm of her chair. Then she stood and walked over to a drawer and took out the old photo of her and Ivo. She touched his face with her finger and she began to talk as if she were alone with him.

I REMEMBER YOUR mother's small herb garden, Ivo, and the smell of thyme and mint. I remember you in the doorway of our old apartment. This is where I first saw you after the war, after so long not knowing if you were alive or dead. I hurried to you and there you were, and you cannot imagine the moment of peace I felt in your arms again. The first night we sat at the kitchen table together, I let you put your hands over mine, touch me, and you began to talk, how I loved your voice, it was a shock to be together. You told me how you used radios to intercept messages, fastened aerials on stop signs, looked for me through the airwaves, you were always good at making things work, always I had watched your hands fixing things, engines, bicycles, the lights in my mother's store, the shingles on my father's shop, always I loved watching you fix things. You were useful in the war, got intelligence, listened to military orders, recorded enemy movement through burned villages and Ivo, you told me how you fell asleep one night and the next day you worried there had been a transmission and you had missed the order and you were starting to go crazy, hearing the things you were hearing, afraid even one more death would be your fault.

Our first night together we were shy though always we have been best friends, telling each other everything, and you hesitated when I began to tell you about Foča. You told me it was

178

you who found the man who bought me and drove me to Tuzla. The night he came to Karaman's I was so terrified, I thought he was taking me away to kill me. It was bad, you said. Yes. There are no decent words. Merima? Oh Ivo. I had always told you everything, but I could not say more. I fell asleep in your arms but there was not even a kiss, and did you want to kiss me, make love to me, would it have healed you? There were so many more things to say and in the night you woke with nightmares, the arm under my neck jerked and my head was tossed to the side and you were not awake and you shouted in your sleep, and then you seemed to be adjusting a headset and you listened and said, Five hundred pieces, finish the job off. Ivan, wake up, you're dreaming, and still you could not see me and you were shouting, Shut up, the emission is still coming through, listen, the job is done. I was crying from across the room, Ivan, wake up and when you finally woke up you sat on the bed and you said, I am sorry, I am so sorry. Never had I seen you cry and it was breaking me and how much more could I be broken?

How destroyed we were.

I still love the image of you so beautiful and tall in our doorway the night you found me again.

In the daytime you listened to the news and I said, Ivo, we need to get water, turn off the news. Everyone was trying to repair the places they lived and you were good at electricity. It had been a surprise to see stop lights and the lights in kiosks when I first arrived in Vienna. We had lived in darkness for a long time. We went out to find food and fresh water and we began to meet those who survived and to learn who died. I was afraid of the night, your country of horror, you were so strong, what if you hurt me when you were asleep and I was not strong enough to get away, always, before the war, when we saw each other after being apart we made love, and still we had not made love. I said to you, Ivo, let's try, and I pretended I felt no pain but it burned like hot glass, and after, you lifted yourself gently from me. You said, I heard your name on their walkie-talkies, I thought I would go crazy, I thought Merima was dead.

I said, You did the best you could.

But your eyes were ashamed and turned away and you said, I am death.

I pleaded with you, However painful life is, it is better than death. Death is nothingness.

You said, Your will to live is insane. Why cling to a life that's finished?

I said, What about our daughter? Tomorrow can we go to her. We will start over in Vienna. What about me? I want to live.

I turned to check that the door was open if I had to run away. I had come to this.

You said, Don't you have enough courage to see you have no future?

You looked out the window and when you turned, your eyes were absent. You said, The generals have destroyed me. I want them murdered by their own flesh and blood. I want them gorged upon.

I was so afraid I might do something, move, make a noise to startle your soul, like pulling the pin on a grenade. I never knew when I might disturb your darkness. It felt like living with a wild animal. You said, There are not enough generals to kill.

I said to you, Do not say this. We can imagine a future.

But you left to walk the streets. I believed that you would come back from the half-dead place. It takes time. I wanted you but my body was always in pain and I did not know what to do. I wanted you, Ivo, I wanted you, even with the nightmares that bled into our days. Sweet Ivo, the generals accomplished their purpose, they destroyed us and they left us alive.

You said when you came home, You are not safe from me in our bed. And I do not know what to do.

I fixed a second sleeping place on the couch near the door. I remembered when we had lived cheerfully in a messy nest of books and papers and cassette tapes and magazines. I said, Ivo, let's go to Vienna, to our daughter. She is waiting to see you.

You said, Soon.

Our home was littered with things we could not speak of. We did not speak of people who had disappeared, your parents, my father, our school friends, the woman who ran the post office, the tobacconist. I told you about old Zedro, the doorman at my law school. The day before Merima and I took the bus to Foča the radio broadcasts were blaring hatred and there were demonstrations. Everyone said it meant nothing, it was only politicians and protests. I was running up the steps into the law building where Zedro sat in the office behind the glass window. He turned off his radio and he said to me, I am not capable of hurting someone's child or setting fire to a friend's house. I would rather die than do the things they are broadcasting. I laughed at him. I said, It's just propaganda. Enjoy your coffee. The next day, when I was waiting for the bus, I heard he had hanged himself. Men were moving trucks of munitions, moving their families away, but our own president was still saying there would not be war.

Ivo, I wanted not to think.

Ivo, what happened to you, gentle, sweet Ivo? We were supposed to travel to Vienna but you went drinking with some men

KIM ECHLIN

and stayed out late, and I fell asleep and our neighbour pounded
on the door in the middle of the night and she was distraught.
She said, Come, see.

Why were you down there, all alone, your drunken friends
gone and where did you get that goat, that poor little goat? You
had tied it on a fence, legs splayed, a rope around the neck, the
poor thing screaming for its life and you were stabbing it with a
kitchen knife, and you were groaning, and you cursed it, and
you cut out its tongue and shouted, Escort of the dead, take me.
I ran down and screamed from across the lot, Ivan! But I stayed
far away I was so frightened. Then the bleating stopped and, no
need to describe, the goat was gone. You sat on the cement,
exhausted, and I said, Ivan, come in, but you would not, you got
up and disappeared into the streets and I locked our door
against you. At noon you appeared again. Now you were dressed
up in borrowed clean clothes, even your hair was cut and you
looked so much like how you once were—only your eyes were
bloodshot. You said, Come walk up the mountain with me, I am
sorry for last night. I am sorry.

Always we had loved to walk up the mountain together. It
was a pretty day and we sat for a while on the bombed-out
foundation of the Osmice hotel and we looked at our city below
and you said, Do you not still love our home? Let's walk along
the bobsled track.

The track was much destroyed in the war. We found the wall
where I had spray-painted beneath your heart *Forever.* I put my
arm around your waist.

You stepped away from me and said, Edina, I cannot go on,
and you put your hand in your pocket and pulled out a grenade
and you said, Come with me.

I could not look away from your finger on the ring. All I could think about was our daughter and I was watching you hook your index finger around the ring, and you said, I'll count to ten.

I knew grenades, ten was not enough, and I ran, I had to make thirty feet and in a moment I do not understand, counting as far as six, I jumped over the bobsled track and fell, in slow motion. Please, please, no land mine on the ground where I fall. These thoughts passed clearly through my head in those six seconds and I remember only silence in the falling, then the click, then darkness. I do not remember the landing or the explosion but I remember the falling and I smelled forest and I saw a bit of sunlight on a pine needle.

She put the photograph back in the drawer.

EDINA SAID, WHEN I woke up, I heard hospital sounds, nurses laughing in a hallway. Kosmos was sitting beside my bed and my first thought was, I am alive.

Anything else was remnant.

She said, Kosmos cried and he said, That crazy bastard. How could he do that? Why the hell do we blow ourselves up?

Edina said, I told him to stop talking and to go write something only in swearing.

He said, I will call it *I Hope Your Cow Dies.*

I was alive in the thin world of the living.

I told Kosmos to leave me alone but he said, One who loves once, loves always. He said, When you are better we will bury Ivan together.

I said, How will I tell Merima? There is nothing to bury.

But there was. We buried Ivan, limbs, his head, in the Širokača and Hambina Carina graveyard in Bistrik so he could be in a high place looking down over the valley.

Now he is another fleck of soldier-dust.

I miss Ivo, she said. Even his enemies will weep when they know what happened to him. I still hear his voice, *Oh god, put me gently to rest without struggle. Let me perish, tell my old father, tell my mother who raised me, tell my beloved. Anything left untold, I myself will tell to the dead in the underworld.*

At least I think this is what Edina said. Her words were indistinct. I had a sensation that the dead were speaking through her, but of this I could not be sure.

I GET UP to write in the cinnabar chill before dawn. But first I will walk through Sibelius Park to the twenty-four-hour grocery store. A long time ago, a small girl disappeared here and was found a few weeks later, her limbs wrapped and bent and hidden in a freezer. In the empty store I choose an apple from the bins, Red Delicious, which Mam calls Hawkeyes, Golden Delicious, McIntosh, and newer kinds, Fuji and Pink Lady and the Honeycrisp to which I am partial. The sleepy clerk has been awake all night.

Above her head, a security camera and grainy, grey images of us on a screen. She lifts her chin off her hand and asks, That all?

Yes, that's all.

Then I go home and write.

I press the words out. To recover is a kind of forgetting. I do not want to forget. The words will not stay in place. Find the correct home in each phrase for each word. The exact common word. The precise formal word. There must be no drama for drama's sake. There must be only correct telling. There *is* a correct word for each feeling. Resist the decay of imprecision. Find the simple word and the clear image, planets in a dark universe.

Only pain resists words. Approach it as a silent supplicant and leave all that you are on a distant shore.

AFTER I FINISHED writing, I stacked the pages on my desk. History changes, like borders. The story changes according to who tells it.

An unexpected storm blew up. Mam was out gliding and sudden winds took her far away. Her wing caught, they said, on a thousand-year-old tree growing from the rock of the escarpment and the fuselage smashed down and snapped like balsa wood. Her jaw and both arms were broken. I almost lost her.

While she was recovering, her arms in casts and her jaw wired shut, I sat with her. Each day the same: wake, get up, lift her, pivot her and slide the legs over the bed, then shift to the front and hold her under the armpits, try not to jostle her. Put her on the commode. Wait, wipe and sponge bathe. Change her clothes and strip the sheets and put them in the wash and prepare her liquid breakfast and hold the straw and then hold her from the back the way I did when Biddy was learning to ice-skate, walk with her across the room because she refused a wheelchair. Keep the legs strong. We devised a primitive system of blinking to talk, one blink for yes and two blinks for no.

On the third day she refused to take the straw. I asked if she wanted a vegetable drink, two blinks, was she in pain, two blinks, did she want the commode, two blinks, did she want to practise walking, two blinks, was she depressed, two blinks, well then what the hell? Her eyes moved and rested on my notebook and pens and I asked if she wanted me to read her what I had written, one blink.

On the telephone that night, I told Edina about reading aloud.

Edina asked, Did she like it?

Who could like such a story. But she likes hearing what I write. We will finish tomorrow.

Edina laughed, I like my daughter's work too. Whatever she does. The daughter redeems the mother's life.

The next day I read to the end. After the testimony of Merima, Mam cried, and I reached over and dabbed her face.

Shall I finish?

One blink.

At the end of the last page I laid the pages down. She raised her eyebrows and the pupils in her eyes opened to hold me.

I said to her that I felt the women who witnessed paid a price, one blink, but that still the women lived on, created themselves again, tried to make life.

Mam's fatigue overwhelmed her and she closed her eyes and dropped into a deep and natural sleep. The twilight was turning the park purple and green, and through the window I saw Biddy hurrying home with her school books, swift and full of intention, and there we all were, suspended in the moment between night and day.

JACQUES PAYAC WAS watching footage of the Labrador Highway in winter. He pointed to his computer screen and said,

The damned owners think we should include links in our articles—terrible word, *links*—to movies, as if words do not do a good enough job.

I laughed and said that they were videos and it was good to see him too and I put a bottle of Scotch on his desk and asked him if he could close up shop for the day. I told him about the end of the trial and the judgment, and he listened like a newsman. He asked what the expert witnesses said about customs of war and how the women withstood the questioning of the defence.

Then he asked, What is next for these women witnesses? Can they accept that one man stands in for all? Can any of us accept this?

I said, Their memories of violence are unlike other kinds of memories. What happened to them cannot be made to seem normal in any way and so it cannot be accepted. Only someone who has lived it can know.

Jacques poured himself a tumbler of Scotch and said, Do you how much a dram is?

No. Is it the same as a shot?

He shook his head and said, No, a dram is 3.6 millilitres and a shot is 44.3 millilitres. A dram is only 1.9 percent of a shot.

He drank down his glass with satisfaction, put it empty on the table and said, I'd rather have nothing than a dram.

He picked up his pen and placed it in a straight line across the top of his desk and said, They wanted to destroy the women and keep them alive. What happens to the women's rage? To their pain?

I had no answer. I did not want to use the word *trauma* because we all think we know what trauma means but I do not think we do.

Can a soul be amputated? I said.

Perhaps, said Jacques. Humans go on living in all kinds of conditions.

He told me about his own mother who lost her memory, and on the last day of her life she stared out the window of her home of sixty years, unable to feed herself, dress herself or go to the toilet. She said to him, Life is precious at the end.

I told him I sometimes wondered whether the experiences of these women would be buried again waiting to be dug up by later generations. I wondered if their words would be released into a future or lost to time.

Jacques Payac said, Violence is with us always. Do not let their words be lost.

Did I tell you about the evidence vaults where they keep the court records? I asked. Rows and rows of white file boxes on metal shelves in the basements. Below the earth. Orders. Telegrams. Radio transmissions. Scraps of rotting cloth, blind-folds, bindings, guns, ammunition. What do such relics mean?

Jacques shifted in his chair. Took off his leg.

I said, Always I have loved being in the world. But their stories. Each woman tells a fragment of that war. The true story and the story of the story must cleave. But there remains shame and silence.

Jacques said, You cannot write all of it.

I said, The women are not words transcribed on a page or images in pel and raster. They are flesh-chained and living. They called for help. No one came.

Jacques balanced his leg against his desk. Leaned back in his chair. He said, No one can undo knowing.

I thought, Locked in a basement vault full of files is the plea of a child, a flower girl at a wedding, Hana. Her mother's moan silenced a courtroom. The transcript reads: *My daughter wanted to live. No one helped her.*

I said, There is only time's erasing. The law carves incisions in old scars and makes a record, and still there is no healing.

Jacques' stump was bothering him and I watched him massage it. I asked him for more work, said I wasn't sleeping well, said I needed money, said I needed to settle down.

He said, Young man, you will not sleep until you write their stories. Get off your ass and put Joe de Pone to work.

I laughed and said, Don't talk to me. I already wrote the story.

He raised his glass.

I asked, Has anyone ever mentioned the disappearance of Joe de Pone's columns?

Not a single person. No one misses him.

Do you think anything makes a difference?

He said, As opposed to nothing? We have to care enough to imagine each other's lives.

I said, Now the law has changed again. But we cannot hold shifting history any better than we can hold water in our hands.

When the law changes, he said, consciousness changes. Allow but a little consciousness.

I said, There are more women and more wars. What about them?

He said, I am thinking of the women you have written about.

There is no solace, I said. There is only forgetting.

He said, Not forgetting. The stories are there.

But it goes on.

He said, I have not forgotten what two light feet on the ground feel like or the touch of a lover on my leg before there was loss and pain. I have not forgotten the stories you have told me. Memory is caught in time. I respect consciousness. But I love time.

Jacques leaned forward and said, I search for connections and I do not always find any. I tell you, war is the common thread. This is not hopeful but it is a fact which I cannot ignore. We know what is happening everywhere, but we do not know what to do. The women came to a cold courtroom in a place on the sea and they spoke. There were many languages and many histories in those rooms and people found ways to listen to each other.

Is that all? I said.

He poured another glass.

He said, What else is there?

I said, The women found words to speak.

He rubbed his stump. Yes, he said.

The women's stories are inscribed inside me, I said. And now they are inscribed inside you.

In order to expose the crime,
you violate the witness.

—*Jadranka Cigelj*

The public and the private
worlds are inseparably
connected; . . . the tyrannies
and servilities of the one are
the tyrannies and servilities
of the other.

—*Virginia Woolf*

This work of fiction is drawn from events at the
International Criminal Tribunal for the Former
Yugoslavia (ICTY). The official transcripts of the Foča
trial, Kunarac et al. (IT-96-23 & 23/1), are in the public
record and available for anyone to read.

All characters and episodes are invented. All names
and identifying numbers of individuals have been
changed. The women who testified deserve their
privacy and our admiration.

I am especially indebted to the thought of Jean Améry
in *At the Mind's Limits*, and to his lived experience and
writing about memory, history, torture, resentments
and the responsibility to know. On page 155, I cite
from Améry directly: *You don't want to listen. Listen
anyhow. You don't want to know to where your indiffer-
ence can again lead you and me at any time? I'll tell you.*

Acknowledgements

Thank you to Bakira Hasečić at the Association of Women Victims of War (Udruzenje Žene-Žrtve Rata) for generous discussions with me and for your courageous work of documentation and legal action; thank you to Diana Dicklich (formerly ICTY) and Iain Reid (formerly ICTY) for your expertise, guidance, reading, friendship and laughter over many years; thank you to Salam Hatibović and Skender Hatibović (Sarajevo Funky Tours: Breaking Prejudice) for sharing your stories; thank you to Milica Kostic (formerly Sites of Conscience), Dita Agoli (formerly ICTY), Hildegard Uertz-Retzlaff (formerly ICTY) for discussion of international activism and law; to Alma Agic (formerly ICTY) and Azra Kovačević (formerly ICTY) and Maxine Marcus (International prosecutor, Human Rights Watch) for expertise; to Janice Blackburn for law questions; to Alison Harvison Young, Jane Springer, Janet Stewart (formerly ICTY), Ken Gass for reading; to Veronica Van Dam for language questions; to Ellen Elias-Bursac for language and interpretation questions; to Sasha Kulic for chess instruction and reading; to Kate Trotter for expertise; to Alketa Xhafa Mripa for your art installations and listening; thank you to Roxana Spicer for a place to work; to Julia Bennett who first told me the story. Thank you to Shaun Oakey for superb editing, Scott Sellers for finding a place in the world for this book. To Hana El Niwairi for your work and enthusiasm. A profound thank you to Nicole Winstanley for your creativity and loyalty, for your love of words and unwavering dedication to what matters. To my family, Ross, Olivia and Sara, thank you for lively discussion and for always being there.

Award-winning author KIM ECHLIN lives in Toronto. She is the author of *Elephant Winter* and *Dagmar's Daughter*, and her third novel, *The Disappeared*, was shortlisted for the Scotiabank Giller Prize, won the Barnes & Noble Discover Great New Writers Award for Fiction and was published in twenty countries. Her most recent novel, *Under the Visible Life*, was critically acclaimed, endorsed by Khaled Hosseini and declared "nothing short of a masterpiece" by *Quill & Quire*.